Loyal to His Love:
Dallas and Morgan
Part 2

A Novel By:
A'Zayler

Text LEOSULLIVAN to 22828 to join our mailing list!

To submit a manuscript for our review, email us at leosullivanpresents@gmail.com

Dallas laid on the ground staring at the men above him. Their eyes were dark with ill intent as the heavy barrels to their guns hovered over his head. Dallas was fighting as hard as he could to stay conscious. He could feel his heart rate slowing down with every breath he took. Writhing in pain on the ground, Dallas thought about all the things that were important to him, and all of the things he'd wanted to do in life. The more he thought, the more agonizing the pain became; it was like his body was succumbing to defeat. He fought hard not to accept the fact that his life was about to end. Out of all the shit he'd done in life, he managed to get caught slipping by two amateur ass niggas. He could tell by the way they were standing around looking at him that they weren't real killers. He should have been dead a long time ago.

If he hadn't been talking to Morgan, he would have saw them coming. Morgan, his sweet beautiful Morgan. She was who he would miss the most. How would she live without him? Hell, how would he go on without her? He couldn't stand being apart from her. Even in death, he wanted her by his side. He wasn't ready—not now, not without her. Thoughts of her clouded his mind so bad that he started to hear her again. For a while her voice had died out, but now it was loud again. She was screaming, but it sounded a little foggy.

"DALLAS! DALLAS! WHERE ARE YOU? DALLAS ANSWER ME!"

Dallas shook his head. He was putting major pressure on his eardrums trying to hear her voice. She was screaming, but she was still far away.

"Morgan, calm down baby," Dallas said.

"Hang up the fucking phone!"

This time, instead of hearing Morgan's voice, he heard one of the gunman's. Dallas shook his head and closed his eyes. When he opened them, he looked around in uncertainty. He was back standing on the side of the hotel with two masked men in front of him. Dallas felt his chest and face, now realizing he'd been daydreaming. Dallas was still on the phone with Morgan, which explained why he could still hear her. His eyes roamed over the two men, taking in the scene.

The one closest to him demanded he hang up the phone. As soon as Morgan heard the voice, she asked who it was.

"Aye baby let me call you back." He didn't even bother to answer her question.

The other gunman decided to taunt Dallas a little.

"Yeah, tell M you'll call her back. She's about to be a little tied up herself."

Upon hearing this, Dallas became furious. He stepped forward, only to be halted by the gun being aimed at his head.

"Y'all mothafuckas better not touch her!"

Brice noticed the instant change in Dallas' mood. "If you cooperate she'll be fine. If not, I'll have my boys blow her fucking head off."

By now, Morgan was irate. She had been yelling and trying to get Dallas to answer her, but he wouldn't. She kept yelling about getting to him before they took him somewhere or hurt him. The moment she'd heard the voices, she'd started yelling. She had been listening for every detail. Dallas was trying to hang up his phone before she could hear anything else; he knew she would try to come look for him.

"I love you. I'll call you later." Dallas hung up the phone.

He glared at the men before asking them what they wanted. Both men had on bandanas that covered their faces; the only things you could see were their eyes and skull caps. He had been so busy on the phone with Morgan that he hadn't even saw them coming. Brice ignored Dallas and began nudging him with the gun. With two guns pointed at him, he followed the men to a black car and got in. Normally he wouldn't have gone anywhere that easy, or without his gun, but he didn't want Morgan getting hurt. He wanted to kick himself for leaving his gun in the truck. They'd made it clear they had somebody on her too; Dallas hoped like hell that was a lie. He had to use everything in him not to lunge at the gunmen. He wanted to kill them, but he had to keep Morgan safe–that was the only thing that mattered to him right then. He couldn't be the reason she lost her life. She was so smart and successful; he couldn't let her life go to waste. Her future was bright, and he wouldn't let her get caught in the crossfire. In his mind, Dallas tried thinking of ways to escape. He was a real nigga, and there was no way he was about to let these amateurs rob him of his life, either.

*****

After Brice got into the front seat and Antoine in the back next to Dallas, they pulled off. The moment they got into the car, Antoine blindfolded him. He and Brice both were surprised at how calm Dallas was being. Marley told them that he would be like that if they mentioned his girl, but they didn't know it would be like this. Brice shook his head. He could almost sympathize with Dallas; only one woman had ever had him like that. He loved her to death, but he'd messed up. Now she was happy with another man. He looked at how composed Dallas was in his rearview mirror; his head was lying back on the seat, and his eyes were closed. To say he was unruffled would be an understatement. *Love will make you do some dumb shit.* Once they took the exit towards the vacant house, Brice texted Marely; he let her know everything had gone smooth, and that they were on their way. He had just put his phone away when Dallas asked them again what their issue with him was. Antoine decided to answer him this time.

"There's somebody that wants to see you."

"Who?"

"Don't worry about that." Antoine hit him across the face with the gun; this drew anger from Dallas, but he remained disconcertingly calm.

*****

Across town, Morgan was pacing her room frantically with her gun and phone. She had called King the moment Dallas hung up. She told him as much of the situation as she knew. He and Jade were on their way to her apartment right then. She had to try to remain calm. She heard the gunman say something about blowing her head off; he'd even said something about being tied up. Morgan was so worried about Dallas that she hadn't given one thought to her own life. She could handle herself–anybody that came in her house thinking otherwise wouldn't make it back out. She had both of her guns loaded, one in her hand the other lying on the bed. She knew King and Jade would be pulling up in a few seconds, so she changed; she wore sweats and a tank top. Before she called Dallas, she had been so tired that she had almost fallen asleep twice; now sleep was the furthest thing from her mind.

The knock on her door startled her from her thoughts. After grabbing her other gun off the bed, she walked to the door with both guns aimed. She saw Jade and King through the peephole. As they walked in, she spoke just before King grabbed her by both shoulders, turning her so that she was facing him.

"What's up Morgan? You alright?"

"Yeah I'm good. Has he called you?" She looked straight ahead, still slightly in a daze.

"Nah, I haven't talked to him since earlier. He said he was headed to the hotel. That's where we'll go first." King was still talking when Jade cut him off.

She told him that whomever had approached Dallas would definitely be gone by now. King already knew that, but he was going to check anyway. After putting on her shoes, Morgan locked up her apartment and they left.

"Yo you've reached D, hit me back." Morgan heard his voicemail for the thousandth time since he'd hung up on her. She had tried calling back a number of times, but there was no answer. Feeling so helpless was becoming annoying, but she was going to find him. She *had* to.

Chapter 1

When she looked, up Brice's sister, Tasheena, saw a tall man come in. There were two women directly behind him. They all wore serious faces, determined even. The man was sexy, and the two women were pretty like models. The sick feeling in her gut let her know they were friends of Dallas. Her heart had begun beating faster.

"How can I help you?" She rubbed her sweaty palms on her pants leg.

"Our friend was here earlier. We have reason to believe something happened to him. Has anyone reported anything?" The thicker short girl talked first.

The taller, thin girl was busy looking out of the window. She looked to be observing what was going on in the parking lot. The man stood in front of the door like a bodyguard. He looked like a killer–a Beautiful killer, but still a killer. She had no doubt he would protect the two women. *What did I get myself into?* She thought before telling them she hadn't seen or heard anything all night. The slimmer girl was at the counter before she could finish her sentence. She wanted to know if they had security cameras. The two pretty faces stared at her awaiting her answer; she was so nervous. When her brother had mentioned helping, she hadn't thought about the consequences. She tried to think of the quickest lie she could.

"Yes, but I can't show them to you. Only the police."

"I am the police, sweetheart." Jade flashed her FBI badge.

The fuck? These people are the fucking police! She was really scared now. She didn't want to go to jail. With an obviously unsteady voice, she informed them that she'd call her manager. If he gave his permission, which she knew he wouldn't, she'd show them the tapes. Before she knew it, she was being yanked over the counter by her hair. For the girl to be so skinny, she had an uncanny amount of strength.

Morgan's chest heaved up and down, and her eyes appeared wild with anger.

"This little bitch is lying. She knows something."

"Oww stop! I don't know anything." Tasheena tried to pry the girl's hands from her head.

"Yes the fuck you do. You better start talking right now." Morgan pulled her further across the counter.

The girl had a death grip on her hair. If felt like she wanted to pull every strand from Tasheena's head, and she probably would have had the man not intervened, telling her to chill out.

"I will snatch this bitch bald if it means finding Dallas."

"Morgan, you can't find Dallas in jail. They've got cameras all over this place. Please calm down." Jade tried to get Morgan to loosen her grip on the girl. It took a few more minutes of convincing before Tasheena felt her feet on the floor again.

Morgan paced the floor with her face set into a deep scowl.

"Jade, this hoe better start talking. I will take her ass outside and kill her."

"I swear, I don't know anything," Tasheena pleaded again.

They weren't getting anywhere with the little service clerk. Morgan decided to take matters into her own hands. She walked behind the desk and looked around to see where the security cameras would be. The girl tried protesting, but was told to shut up instantly.

"It's nothing back there. Let's go look around outside." Morgan didn't bother waiting for an answer from Jade or King. King followed her out the door, but Jade stayed behind. She leaned over the counter and stared at the girl.

"You better hope nothing happens to my brother and you knew about it. I'm going to personally come back here and arrest you for conspiracy. Only *after* I let my sister beat your ass." She gave a polite smile before joining King and Morgan outside.

They looked around the entire building for what seemed like hours. Even after talking to patrons and checking with the security guards, they still came up with nothing. The only thing they'd found that had been helpful was that some of the cameras had been cut.

King was furious.

"The cameras were only out on this side. This had to be where they were."

"This was a set up. I got the right mind to go in there and drag that little receptionist out. I could beat her ass until she tells the truth." Morgan ran her hands through her hair before starting towards the front of the building again; Jade pulled her back.

"Nah Morgan, don't beat her up because then she can file charges. We can go back in there and scare her ass until she starts talking."

Morgan looked around the parking lot as she contemplated what Jade said; that was when she spotted Dallas' truck. She told King and Jade before running towards it. Disappointment set in when she realized it was locked. If Morgan thought she was mad, King was worse. It was like seeing Dallas' truck sent him over the edge. He walked away, seething as he cursed violently. A few moments later, she heard him say Smoke's name while on the phone. That calmed her a little, because between the two of them, they'd make something happen. She looked at King on the phone again before she pulled Jade back towards the front of the hotel. Morgan pulled her gun out of her waist band.

● ● ●

14

Jade tried to get Morgan back to rational thinking, but she wasn't listening. After Morgan told her she would be the exact same way if this were King, Jade got quiet and followed her into the building. When they entered, the lobby was empty. The only person there was the girl.

*****

When Tasheena saw the gun in the girl's hand, she got nervous. She had tried calling Brice a few times, but he hadn't answered. She really didn't want to tell on her brother, but she didn't want to die or go to jail either. The slim girl placed her gun on the counter before talking.

"I'll ask you one more time. Do you know anything about what went on here with my boyfriend tonight?"

"All I know is two guys came in here and paid me to cut the cameras off on the left side. They said they were about to rob somebody. They didn't say anything about taking him."

Jade leaned towards her. "So you saw their faces?"

"Yeah they were both brown-skinned and medium height with all black on. They had low haircuts."

"So it was two of them?" Tasheena nodded her head yes at the girl that had shown her the badge. The skinny girl stood back, snatched her gun off the counter, and pointed it at her.

"Why the fuck didn't you say that shit when we first came in here?"

Tasheena held both of her hands up in surrender. "They said they would come back and kill me if I said anything."

Morgan pointed her gun at the girl's chest. "What the fuck you thought I was about to do?"

Tasheena begged for her life as tears ran down her face. Her body was shaking nervously as her breaths got heavier. Jade demanded that she go get the tapes. She ran to the back in a hurry and came back with two tapes, because she wanted to diffuse the situation. They were from last week, but she handed them to them anyway.

"They had on black with low haircuts." She was basically talking to their backs as they exited the building again.

She was wrong for lying, but she would never rat her brother out. She had just recently found out she even had a brother. After her fiancé was killed in a home invasion, she had to get out of town and get a fresh start. She had moved from Virginia to GA to stay with her father for a little while, only to find out she had an older brother as well. Brice was so nice and welcoming; she loved him immediately. At first she hadn't wanted to help him with this, but she figured it would make them closer. She tried calling him again, but it went to voicemail. This time she texted him, letting him know he needed to call her ASAP.

*****

"Here are the tapes from today." Jade handed them to King.

"Alright, let's go watch them and see if we recognize anybody." King walked towards his truck. Morgan's eyes began to water when she looked back at Dallas' truck. What would she do if they couldn't find him?

"Yo Morgan, I'll drive you back to your house so you can get you some clothes and Dallas' truck keys. We're going to come back and pick up his truck, then you're staying at the house until we figure this shit out."

There was no argument from either of the girls. Morgan tried to keep her sobs quiet as she looked out of the window.

*****

Inside the house, Dallas lie on the floor unconscious. Brice and Antoine had followed Marley's instructions and beat him up pretty bad. Brice felt bad about it, but Antoine could care less; all he cared about was getting paid. During the beat down, Antoine had even picked up a bat and hit him a few times. Brice stopped him after he saw him hit Dallas in the back of the head with it. He had no beef with Dallas, so he didn't want to kill him. He wanted to hold up his end of the deal, get his money, and part ways with Marley.

"She still ain't hit you back yet?" Antoine looked at Brice.

"Nah, I told her we were on our way. She was supposed to meet us over an hour ago."

Antoine laughed when he looked at Brice. "This bitch better not try to fuck us over with our money. I'll beat her ass the same way we just did this nigga."

Brice didn't find anything funny; honestly, he wished he could take back agreeing to do it. He didn't even know this dude, and he had no real beef with him. Once he saw him in the light, he had even recognized him, he just couldn't remember from where. After racking his brain trying to place his face, he got irritated and called Marley again. He left her another voicemail before placing his phone down. Trying to take his mind off of Marley, he decided to call his sister back. She had called a few times and texted, but he figured she was just scared. When she said hello, he could hear the panic in her voice.

"Brice, some people came by here looking for him. They asked about y'all." She was whispering, so he could tell she was still at work. She went on and on about being afraid because she didn't know whether they were coming back or not; that made him sit up.

"Who were they? What did they look like? Did they say their names or anything?"

"They were his friends, I know one of them was his girlfriend because she said it."

Brice cursed as he scratched his head.

"Her name was Morgan. She called the other girl Jade. The man never said his name."

Brice thought his heart was about to stop. *Jade?* At that moment, he knew where he'd recognized this dude from.

"Bam!" His sister called him by his nickname, getting his attention.

He had completely zoned out, realizing what he had just done. Jade was his ex, the one girl he loved, and Morgan was her best friend. Dallas was Jade's new man's best friend, and Morgan's boyfriend. He had almost robbed him one time before for that nigga Trapp, but Morgan had put a stop to that shit. It all hit him like a ton of bricks. How did he let Marley get him involved in something like this? He let out a loud breath as he banged his head against the wall. He could hear his sister asking what was wrong, while Antoine looked on in confusion.

"I know these people, sis."

"Dang. For real Brice?"

"Yeah, let me hit you back. Go home before they come back. They are not people you want to play with."

"I know. The Morgan girl pulled her gun on me, and Jade threatened to arrest me."

"Fuck man. Go home Tasheena, I'll meet you there." He ended their call.

King's little brother Jaden had told BamJade was a fed now. He was proud of her then, but now that shit could blow up on him. Bam didn't think she would arrest him, but then again if this nigga died, she just might.

Brice got up off the floor. "Antoine, I'm about to bounce. This bitch isn't answering her phone, then I just found out this my ex peoples right here. I got to go."

Antoine looked at Dallas' motionless body as he got off the floor too. He asked Bam would Marley fuck them over, but he said no–for her sake, she'd better not. Antoine wouldn't hesitate about going to see her.

"She has my number, and everything I ever discussed with her was over the phone. No text messages, so as far as me and you are concerned, we didn't have nothing to do with this shit."

Antoine was glad to hear that. He checked Dallas' neck for a pulse; it was light, but it was there. After looking around and making sure there was nothing else there that belonged to them, they closed the door and left the house. Bam contemplated about calling the police, but he didn't want this to lead back to them, so he decided against it. Dallas was unconscious, so he couldn't point any of this back to them right now, as far he was concerned, their hands were clean. He dropped Antoine off first, then headed to his home.

It had been three days, and Marley hadn't bothered to call Brice back yet. She figured she'd wait them out just in case they went to the local police. She did that because she trusted Brice, but not his friend. She didn't know him, so she steered clear for a few days. Marley got out of bed and got dressed. She decided she would go by the house and check to see if Dallas was still there. Her date with Neko would keep her occupied until then. She had been using him to keep her busy for the last couple of weeks, but she was ready to get rid of him; tonight would be the night she ended things. Once she pretended to find Dallas, everything would be the way she'd planned, and they could be together. Although he was getting on her nerves, Neko hadn't been a total waste of time. The house that she'd told Brice to put Dallas in was on the same street as Neko's house. She had seen it one day on her way home and knew it would be perfect. No one lived there, and it looked a little run down. The front window was busted and the grass was high–two obvious signs of vacancy. Marley checked the mirror to make sure she looked presentable before she grabbed her purse, shades, and keys, and left the house.

Chapter 2

The last couple of days without Dallas had been hell on Earth for Morgan. She had looked day and night for him, and between her, King, and Smoke, they had searched the entire city. Exhausted was an understatement for the way she felt physically and mentally. She had called out of work and spent all of her time trying to find him. Last night she had built up enough nerve to call hospitals and local morgues to check for any unidentified African American males; thank God there weren't any. With her head in her hands, she began to cry again. It was all she had been able to do lately, and she was growing very tired of it.

"You okay Morgan?" King was standing at the door of his and Jade's guest room.

Morgan had been staying there since the night of Dallas' disappearance. More tears ran down her cheeks as she shook her head no. King walked in and sat down next to her on the bed. He wrapped his arm around her shoulder and pulled her to him. She continued to cry with her face pressed into his shoulder.

"Everything will be alright, Morgan. Dallas is a fighter; wherever that nigga is, I can bet you he's giving their asses hell."

King had been stressing about Dallas too. He'd been trying to keep it together for Morgan; if he lost hope, so would she. They had to find Dallas soon. There was no way she could take much more of this.

"What If he's dead King?" She began crying a little harder.

"I doubt that's the case. Let's cross that bridge when we get there."

"Okay, you're right." She wiped her face, trying to stop the tears. "I think I'ma go to work today. I need to put my mind somewhere else."

King stood to his feet and headed for the door. "Alright. I'm headed out to work too. Call me or Jay if you need anything."

*****

"Baby, you want to come in and watch a movie?" Neko had just gotten out of Marley's car.

"Not today. I got some more stuff I need to handle. I'll just come by tomorrow."

"Alright then, be safe and call me when you get home." He kissed her through her window.

As she backed out of his driveway, Marley tried calling Bam again. He answered dryly.

"Hey Brice, I've been trying to call you."

"Just like I was trying to call you and you hadn't bothered to answer."

"I know. I'm sorry, I've just been busy. I haven't even had time to call his friends for ransom money." Marley wanted to make it known that he and Antoine wouldn't be getting paid for their services. She'd thought about it and decided that part of the plan was a bit much.

"Whatever Marley. This shit is dead anyway. Fuck the money and don't worry, we're not snitching. You're on your own with this. We're done."

She was past angry now. She was sure he could hear the attitude in her voice when she asked where Dallas was.

"What you mean where is he? You never went to check on him?" Bam practically yelled in shock.

"No, I'm headed there now." She hung up the phone.

*****

Bam couldn't believe Dallas had been in that house for three days. He was probably dead by now, but he hoped he wasn't—not just because he was Jade's friend, but because he hadn't done anything to deserve this. Marley was just crazy as hell. Bam bowed his head and said a silent prayer for Dallas. He turned the basketball game back up—this was Marley's problem now.

*****

After slowing her car to a stop in front of the vacant house, Marley got out and went in. She didn't see Dallas until she walked around the corner. He was lying in the middle of the floor badly beaten and bruised. He looked so lifeless that she was scared to get close to him.

When she eased closer, she noticed he still had a blindfold on.

"Help me," she heard him say barely above a whisper. *YES!* She thought to herself; now was the perfect time for her to come into play.

"Oh my God! Dallas, what happened to you?" She snatched the blindfold off.

He squinted his swollen eyes to look at her and asked for help again.

"Okay Dallas, I'm about to call 911." She scooted closer and laid his head in her lap.

Her hand shook as Neko's voice startled her. "Marley what the fuck you doing in here?"

When she saw him standing at the front door, she put on her best performance.

"Thank God you're here Neko! I saw two men running out of here when I was driving past. I heard one of them say something about leaving the man inside, so I got out. I know it was stupid of me, but now I'm glad I did—it's Dallas."

She tried hard to maintain the tears in her eyes. Neko rushed over to them and snatched his cell phone out of his pocket. He called 911, gave them the address, and began checking Dallas for any deadly wounds.

"Thank God he's not shot or stabbed, but whoever did this beat the fuck out of him." Neko examined the bruises on his face and body. Dallas wore nothing but a bloody T-shirt and some basketball shorts.

One of his legs was swollen and purple; he had obviously been beaten with something. It pained him to see his boy like that; Dallas was truly a good person.

"Damn Dallas, did you see who did this?" Neko could hear the sirens coming up the street. Dallas shook his head so softly Neko barely saw it move.

"Who would do something like this?" Marley continued to fake cry.

"I don't know, but we are most definitely going to find out. When we do, I hate it for 'em.'"

Neko got up to go outside to the paramedics. The short male EMT asked where Dallas was; Marley cringed when she heard Neko say he was in the living room with his girlfriend.

*****

Morgan's pager went off as she walked down the halls of Emory. She checked it and went to the nurses' station. The older nurse handed her the phone letting her know she had a call.

"He said it's an emergency."

She answered it in a hurry, hoping it was Dallas.

"Hey Morgan, its Neko. I found Dallas."

Morgan's breath was caught in her throat as she prepared herself for what was next. "Is he alive?"

"Barely, he was in an abandoned house. Somebody almost beat him to death. We're headed to Emory right now. I was hoping you were there."

"I'm here. Bring him. I'll be waiting for you in the ER." She snatched her cell phone from her pocket and dialed Jade.

"Hey Jay, call King and let him know they found him. He's on the way to my job now. I'm at Emory. I'll fill you in once y'all get here," she said before Jade could even say hello.

Jade let her know that she and King would be there shortly and hung up. Morgan took off full speed; she ran through the hospital until she reached the emergency room. She gained a few agitated stares from people in the hallways, but she didn't care–she had to get to Dallas. Emory was a huge hospital, but she had to be there when they brought Dallas in.

Finally outside, she waited for the ambulance to pull up. Not even a full five minutes later, it flew around the corner and stopped right in front of her. The doors popped open and out came Marley and Neko. Marley caught her off guard for a second, but she quickly pushed her out of the way; she needed to get next to Dallas. The sight of him made her sick to her stomach. He was so beat up she almost didn't recognize him.

"Dallas!" When she screamed, his eyes fluttered before closing again "Dallas baby!" She ran alongside the paramedics. He moved his mouth, but nothing came out.

With no sounds being heard, he reached out his hand to her.

The paramedic next to her began to tell the doctors what was going on with him. "We have a male in his mid-twenties. He's severely dehydrated, beaten, with an injury to the back of his head. He also appears to have an infection in his right leg."

"Morgan, we're going to have to ask you to move." The doctor grabbed her shoulder. By the hysterical cries coming from Morgan, it was clear that she knew the patient.

"No I'm staying here with him." She was very forceful with her answer. Morgan knew the doctor and respected her tremendously, but now was not the time; they needed to know she wasn't going anywhere. The doctor then ignored Morgan and gave Dallas her full attention. The moment everyone started working on him, he went into shock. He began bucking and mumbling for them to stop. He wasn't cooperating at all, which could make any injury he had a lot worse. Having seen this type of behavior before in similar situations, Morgan ran to his aid. If he didn't stop, they were going to restrain him, and she didn't want that. She laid the entire top part of her body lightly on top of his, and grabbed his face with both of her hands.

"Dallas. Dallas listen to me. You have to calm down baby," Morgan was trying to get his attention. She could tell by the bewildered look on his face he didn't know where he was.

"Dallas calm down baby. I'm right here with you." When she noticed he was starting to relax a little, she repositioned her body to keep him from moving and continued talking. "It's me Morgan. You're hurt really bad, and you're at the hospital. You have to calm down and be still. I'm right here with you. I love you." She rubbed the sides of his face and whispered softly to him until they were able to get him sedated.

She was trying her hardest not to cry, but it was impossible. He looked so scared. She had never seen him like that. He kept his eyes fixed on her, and they never moved. When she started crying, she saw tears roll down the side of his face as well. They had gotten him stable a few moments later, and she was able to move.

"You have to leave now ma'am. We need to take him to surgery." The doctor pushed Morgan outside of the curtain and into Neko's arms. "Keep her here." The doctor walked away after that.

The state Dallas was in had Morgan lightheaded. The room began to spin before everything went completely black. It was a good thing Neko was holding her, because she had passed out. Watching Neko pick Morgan up and care for her made Marley's blood boil. She didn't want Neko, but she sure as hell didn't want him all over Morgan's ass.

"Excuse me, we need another bed–she just passed out," Neko yelled across the emergency room; Jade rushed to him. She and King had just walked in the door when he yelled for a nurse.

"She passed out after seeing D." He laid Morgan down on the bed the nurse had just brought to them. Jade and King both asked was it that bad, and they learned that Morgan passing out was not a good sign for Dallas' wellbeing.

"Yeah, Dallas is fucked up. They said somebody beat him with a bat or a pipe or something."

"FUCK!" Everybody in the waiting room looked over when King yelled.

Jade grabbed his arm and continued pressing Neko for information. She wanted to know where he was, and who had found him. When he said Marley's name, Jade's eyes began to roll.

"Who?" Jade was unable to hide her attitude, but she needed clarification.

"Marley. She had just left my house and she saw two dudes running from inside of another house. They were saying some shit about leaving the nigga in the house, so she went in, and that's how she found him."

Jade turned around with her eyes trained on Marley; she didn't say anything, she just stared for a minute. She didn't trust that hoe not one bit. Given the situation, she was grateful for her finding him, so she decided not to say anything. She'd stay off of her ass, but she still wasn't about to say thank you. When she finally turned back around, she let King and Neko know that she would stay with Morgan. They agreed to keep her updated on Dallas before she walked towards the back room where Morgan had been taken. By the time she had gotten into the room, Morgan was awake but talking a little slower due to the sedatives they had given her.

"Is Dally okay?"

"I don't know, girl. They were still working on him. Neko said somebody beat him with a bat or a pipe or something." Jade waved her hand as she tried to remember.

"I know. They said he had an infection in his leg and an injury to the back of his head when they first brought him in." Morgan felt herself feeling a little faint, so she laid back down. "Head injuries are serious, Jay. He could die."

"I know Morgan, but Dallas is strong. He's not going to let this keep him down." Jade climbed on the bed with Morgan. The two friends lay there, lost in their own thoughts, when the nurse knocked and came in.

"Morgan Taylor?" He looked at both women, unsure of who was who.

Morgan raised her arm. He informed her that she'd passed out in the emergency room and he needed to check on her. Once she told him she felt better, he turned to leave. He looked at his chart one more time and turned back around facing them.

"We're going to have to do an ultrasound to make sure everything is fine with your baby as well."

"Hold up, wait! With my what?" She and the nurse both wore confused looks.

"Your baby. I take it you didn't know you were pregnant."

"And you would be right." Morgan laid her head back down on the pillow. Jade knew this was a lot for Morgan to take in, so he told the nurse to send the ultrasound tech in.

"Mommy Morgan." Jade rubbed Morgan's stomach.

"Shut up Jade."

"What Jade got to shut up for?" Lay-Lay looked at them as she walked into the room. When they looked up, both girls smiled at Lay-Lay, but only Jade answered.

"Because mommy Morgan doesn't want to accept the fact she's a preggy now."

"Shut the fuck up Jade! For real?" Lay-Lay beamed.

"Yep, we're about to be aunties." Jade and Lay-Lay both were happy.

Lay-Lay noticed Morgan really didn't share in the excitement. She asked Morgan why, and when she answered, she completely understood. Morgan was scared; she didn't know whether Dallas was going to live or die. Lay hugged her best friend as she continued to cry; she told her everything would be alright, even though she wasn't sure she believed it herself. After talking and getting themselves together, the ultrasound tech came in and began the ultrasound.

"Why does the heartbeat sound like that?" Jade looked at the nurse as she waited for an answer.

Morgan sat up to look at the screen. "Yeah it does sound kind of weird. Is everything okay?"

"The heartbeats are perfectly fine. What you ladies hear are two hearts beating together."

She smiled at a puzzled face Morgan. It seemed as if the screen popped up right after she said it, displaying two babies. She circled each baby and labeled them Twin A and Twin B. Jade and Lay-Lay both screamed in excitement. Lay jumped up and down, screaming that she didn't have to share with Jade because they could each get a baby. Jade's eyes bulged as she thought about it. She was so excited that she couldn't wait. Morgan, on the other hand, couldn't stop crying.

"Oh Lord help me."

Jade looked at Morgan with her nose turned up. "Doctor, how far along is she? I don't know how much more of this crying I can take."

"She is 13 weeks along. Everything looks perfect." When Morgan heard the lady say her babies were fine, she calmed down a little. She hadn't been acting very pregnant lately. She'd had drinks on a few occasions and not one doctor's appointment. *Thank you Jesus,* Morgan said in her head.

Chapter 3

On the elevator to the ICU floor, Morgan shifted nervously. Dallas had just gotten out of surgery and they needed to speak with her. When she got off the elevator, she stepped into a waiting room full of people. She smiled and kept walking. At the end of the hall, she saw a short, brown-skinned lady with a long braid going down her back talking to a doctor. The doctor noticed her and smiled. The lady he was talking to turned around as well. The two women exchanged smiles, and the older lady turned back around.

"Hi Dr. Chin. You needed to see me?" She stopped next to the lady.

He briefly placed his hand on Morgan's shoulder. "Yes Morgan dear, how are you?"

"I'm fine now. I just needed a minute to rest."

"You're Morgan?" The lady faced her with a tear stained face. Morgan forced a smile for the woman. She looked like she was going through something major, but so was Morgan.

"Yes mam. I'm a nurse here, how are you?"

She told her she was fine and she'd had them page her. She explained to Morgan that she wanted her to be her son's nurse, but right now wasn't a good time. Morgan got personal requests all the time from returning patients, but that wasn't happening today. She had an agenda, and taking care of anybody outside of Dallas wasn't on it. Morgan politely declined, letting her know there was another patient that would need her around the clock. She offered to get her another nurse, but the lady was firm in her decision.

"No Morgan. I want you. He needs you." Tears slid down her cheeks.

After seeing how adamant the lady was, she obliged; she would check on her son real quick then leave. After all, she was still at work.

"Okay ma'am, show me where he is."

She grabbed Morgan's hand and held it. The lady led them to the ICU door and waited to be buzzed in. She walked around the nurse's desk, and stopped at one of the rooms. She slid the door open. His room was dark, but Morgan would recognize that face anywhere.

"Oh Dally." She rushed to his bedside and kissed all over his swollen face. Looking up with puffy eyes, Morgan made eye contact with Dallas' mom. She was crying as well, but smiling at the same time.

"It's nice to meet you, Morgan."

"I am so sorry. I had no idea who you were." Morgan rushed around the bed to hug her.

"I know. I didn't know what you looked like either. That's why I had them to page you. I just remembered Dallas telling me you worked here."

"Yes ma'am. I would have been with him, but I passed out when I saw him in the emergency room." Morgan took a seat in the chair next to his bed.

She was going to have to get a grip, because all of the crying she was doing was maddening. Double the baby must have meant double the hormone as well. Dallas' mom walked over to where Morgan was sitting and grabbed her hand. She squeezed it lightly as she held it.

"It's fine sweetheart. We're here now."

"Mrs. Streeter, do you mind if I go talk to the doctor and see what's going on?"

"Oh no baby, please do. Call me Marcy." She smiled and let Morgan's hand go.

Morgan looked at Dallas and sighed as she left the room. When she got back to the nurse's station, she saw her friend Amber. She and Amber had started at Emory at the same time. They did most of their training together and had remained friends ever since. She asked about Dallas' surgery and for his chart. Amber forked over the information with no hesitation. She told Morgan Dr. Fitzgerald had done his surgery; that made Morgan happy. Dr. Fitzgerald was the best neurosurgeon in GA; he was highly requested. If Dallas had to have brain surgery, she was happy he'd been the one to do it. When Morgan opened the chart, her heart almost stopped. With her back pressed against the wall, she slid down and sat on the floor. It seemed like the more she read, the weaker her knees got. By the time she had finished reading, she was crying once again.

"This can't be happening."

She leaned her head back against the wall and prayed for Dallas and her babies. The stress their father's condition was putting on her couldn't be healthy for them. After another thirty minutes, Morgan had regrouped herself and had her game face on. She was tired of crying, and tired of being weak. Her dad would kill her if he'd been able to see her the last couple of days. Standing to her feet, she fixed her scrubs and walked back into Dallas' room. She asked Marcy how was she, and if she could get her anything; Marcy said she was fine. Morgan stopped short in her steps when Marcy asked had she learned anything regarding Dallas' condition. She explained they'd told her some stuff, but nothing concrete yet.

"They haven't told me anything yet, either. They're probably trying to monitor him for the next few hours to be sure of what's going on before they tell us. Since I work here, I looked in his chart." She paused, giving Marcy a minute to prepare herself for what she was about to say. "He was beaten pretty badly with something. They're thinking a bat or a steel rod. Either way, it fractured a few of his ribs, broke his wrist, and fractured his skull which, in return, caused his brain to swell, and he has a terrible infection in his right leg."

Marcy was thrown back by the news. She asked Morgan to explain it to her further, in a way she could understand. The doctors had been throwing medical terminology at her all day.

"Because his brain was swollen, they had to cut a piece of his skull out to relieve some of the pressure. This could cause memory loss. The infection in his leg came from being hit with the object. The force of the object damaged his blood vessels, which caused permanent damage to the tissue. The doctors were able to treat it before it spread to his entire body. They've put him in a medically induced coma to give him time to heal." Morgan's voice broke with tears. Quickly wiping the tears in her eyes away, she finished. "Mrs. Marcy I want you to know, he could wake up normal, or he could wake up not remembering anything. In time his memory will return, but the leg infection is aggressive and may need continuous treatment." Marcy screamed placing a hand over her heart.

"Who would do this to him, Morgan?"

"I don't know. I'm going to find out, and when I do, I'm going to personally take care of it. You have my word."

Morgan spent the rest of the day in and out of Dallas' room. She was waiting for him to wake up. After the doctors had come earlier that day and told them pretty much the same thing Morgan had already said, Mrs. Marcy was inconsolable. Morgan was worried, but she was more worried about finding the people who had done this. When she finished her shift on her floor, Morgan went back up to check on Dallas. She wanted to look in on him before she left to grab a change of clothes. Morgan didn't plan on leaving the hospital again until he woke up. She scanned her badge, the doors opened, and she headed for Dallas' room. Inside were his mom, stepdad, and King. His parents had been there all day, and King for the last two hours. She asked had anything changed, only for his stepfather to tell her no.

Willie Streeter was Dallas' stepfather, but the only real father he knew. His dad had left his mom when he was younger. The way Dallas talked about him and the way he was all over Dallas right now, you'd never guess Willie wasn't his biological father. After checking his monitors and his chart for changes, she stood next to the bed and held his hand. Some of the swelling had gone down, but bruises still adorned his face and arms. There was also still a bandage wrapped around his head. Morgan turned to his parents.

"I'm about to run home and grab some clothes. Have y'all made reservations anywhere yet?"

His stepfather shook his head. "No, we've been here all day. We haven't stopped to do much of anything."

"If you want, I can take you to Dallas' house, or you all can stay at my condo. The choice is yours."

Marcy smiled. Morgan was truly a sweetheart. She told her staying at Dallas' house would be fine. She and Willie began gathering their things. As they left, King told them to call him if they needed anything. He loved his aunt and uncle, and wanted their stay to be as pleasant as possible given the situation. Morgan kissed Dallas' cheek before heading out with everyone else. She was going to make her trip quick. She didn't want him to wake up alone.

*****

It had been all day and she still hadn't had a chance to see Dallas yet. When she first got to the hospital, he was rushed off into surgery, and Morgan had been hovering ever since. Marley's eyes rolled as she pressed the ICU door button and waited to be let in. After a few seconds, the door buzzed and she headed towards the nurses' station.

"Hi, I'm looking for Dallas Streeter." She leaned over the desk with a polite smile.

"He's in room 12, but visiting hours are over. Only family is allowed now."

"I am family. I'm his fiancé."

That statement caught Amber's attention. She knew for a fact the patient in room 12 was Morgan's boyfriend. Amber turned completely around to get a good look at Marley. She made a mental note to inform Morgan later. Against her better judgment, she allowed her to go on back. After sliding the door closed behind her, Marley sat her purse down and walked to his bed. She whispered in his ear, telling him to wake up. When he didn't move, she began rubbing up and down his arm. She started to feel bad as she observed how bad of shape he was in. He was going through all of this because of her jealous territorial ways. Yeah, it was for her job too, but she had to admit it was more personal than anything. All she wanted was for him to love her again. Now she didn't even know if he would ever get that opportunity. Her eyes watered up and she began to cry.

"I'm so sorry Dallas," she sniffed, unaware that Morgan had just entered the room.

"What the fuck you sorry for?" She jumped; Morgan's presence had startled her.

"Morgan, you scared me."

Morgan didn't look the least bit fazed by Marley's comment. Instead, she leaned back on one leg and crossed her arm. Her gaze was icy and unwavering.

"Like I said, what are you sorry for?"

Marley began acting her butt off. She said any and everything she could think of. She started from his current condition and went all the way back to breaking up with him in high school. She let out a few tears as she put on her show. She deserved an Oscar for her performance. She had to make sure Morgan believed what she was saying. She had seen Morgan in action before, and she most definitely didn't want any parts of that.

"Whatever girl. Kill the drama. I still don't like your sneaky ass." Morgan finally put her book bag down. Still holding her motorcycle helmet, she walked over to Dallas and kissed his lips before sitting in the chair next to his bed.

"So tell me how you found him again." Morgan leaned back to get a better look at Marley.

"I'm sure you know by now Neko and I have been kicking it for a while. When I was leaving his house, I saw two boys running out of this abandoned house on his street. They both had guns and were yelling. I rolled my window down. When I heard one of them say something about leaving that nigga in the house, I decided to park and see what was going on."

"So you mean to tell me you were just going to go in the house without knowing who was inside or what was going on?"

Marley tried to assure Morgan she just wanted to make sure no one was hurt. Morgan rolled her eyes, and Marley was getting angrier by the second.

*****

Morgan's gut instincts were telling her Marley was lying, but she had no serious proof. For now, she would just keep her as a person of interest.

"Okay, well visiting hours are over now. You are more than welcome to leave."

Morgan was trying to dismiss Marley, but she wasn't having it. She told Morgan she'd leave in a minute. Morgan chuckled lightly before letting her know that she was leaving right then. Morgan didn't care who Marley thought she was. She was Dallas' woman, and anything she said went. Marley rolled her eyes and let out a loud sigh as she got up. She retrieved her purse and left without even looking back. Before the door could close all the way, Amber came in. She informed Morgan of Marley's lies about being Dallas' fiancé. Morgan couldn't believe the nerve of this chick. Morgan let Amber know who Marley really was and thanked her for looking out. Amber winked and went back to the nurse's station. Morgan sat on the side of Dallas' bed and leaned down until her forehead touched his.

"Baby, you had me worried to death looking for you. I'm so glad you're back now. I just wish you would wake up and smile at me or something. I miss you so much, and I have a surprise for you." She paused for a moment before continuing. "I'm pregnant D, we're having twins."

For a long moment she was tempted to cry, but she refused to. She had cried enough; now it was time to make things happen. She pulled out her phone and dialed a familiar number. As soon as the loving deep voice of her father came over the phone, she smiled.

"Hey Daddy. I need your help."

"What's going on, daddy baby?"

She smiled at her pet name. She wasted no time sharing the details about her boyfriend being kidnapped. She told him how bad he was messed up, which peaked his interest. He immediately asked how bad it was. Morgan explained the brain injuries that could possibly cause memory loss; she had to fight back tears in order to finish her story. Upon hearing her sniffles, he asked was she alright. Morgan could hear the sincere sympathy in his voice. Her tears stopped, and a laugh escaped when he offered to fly down to Georgia. The urgency in his voice let her know he'd be on the first thing smoking if she said yes. From the time she was little to now, her daddy would be the first one running anytime she would cry. It took a few attempts to let him know she was fine and he could stay put. Once her voice had gotten back to normal, so did his. He switched right back into serious mode.

"Okay sweetheart. What do you need my help with?"

She loved that about her dad; he was so versatile. He would go from killer to marshmallow just for her.

"Okay, there's this girl that was working at the hotel the night Dallas was taken. She claimed two guys came in and made her cut the tapes. I'm sure that was a lie." Morgan looked over her shoulder at Dallas before continuing.

Arlington cleared his throat. "What makes you so sure?"

"She gave us some tapes and told us they were from that night. After we watched them, we realized they weren't. When I went back to check with her again, her manager said she'd quit."

It took no time for her father to realize what she was asking. He knew she needed the identity of the girl. Morgan had to hold in her excited squeal after his next statement.

"Aright daddy baby, give me about two days and I'll have something for you. What's the name of the hotel and where is it?"

She told him it was the W downtown and prepared to end the call. He said he loved her, and for her to call if she needed anything. After sitting her phone on the charger, Morgan let the bed out on the couch and prepared to get some sleep. She was sure it wouldn't be much, but she had to at least try.

• • •

46

*****

This was definitely not what Arlington Taylor was expecting to hear. He'd known Morgan had been dating Dallas for some time now, but this was a shock. He'd known Dallas pretty much his entire life, and would have never guessed he and Morgan would be an item. Dallas was a good kid, so he approved from afar. He'd never tell Morgan he knew Dallas, because as far as Dallas knew, he didn't. Dallas knew nothing about him, and that's how it would stay. Hearing Dallas had been attacked didn't sit well with him at all. There were some calls that needed to be made. The situation they were in was a weird one, but it worked. Until the time was right, Morgan and Dallas would remain oblivious to his knowledge. Although this was disturbing a lot of the things he had going on, Morgan was his daughter; he would help her in any way possible.

Chapter 4

"Hey Morgan, they need you in ICU," a nurse said as she passed Morgan going up the stairs. This made her stomach drop; she needed to see if it was bad or not before going.

"Did they say why?" The nurse shook her head no and kept walking.

Morgan made a U-turn and headed for the elevators. Once on the floor, she bumped into Marcy. They talked for a few moments, exchanging Dallas stories before Morgan continued on her way. Morgan walked into Dallas' room and got a major surprise. He was sitting up in his bed with his eyes open. Morgan almost slipped and fell trying to get to him. She smiled and yelled his name, but to her dismay he frowned.

"He's not speaking yet, but he can recognize the people around him. I had him nod when asked certain questions. He did surprisingly well for a person recovering from a brain injury," the nurse explained. Morgan decided to try her luck. She grabbed his hand and asked did he know who she was. This time, instead of frowning, he simply shook his head no. Morgan thought she had prepared herself just in case this happened, but she hadn't and it hurt. Marcy had just walked in.

"This is Morgan Dallas, you don't remember her?"

Looking from his mom to Morgan he shook his head no again. This time, Morgan couldn't take it and left the room. She found a quiet room off from the nurses' station and cried. She pulled out her phone and called Jade. She answered on the first ring.

"Jay, he doesn't remember me," Morgan cried into the phone.

"What? What do you mean he doesn't remember you? You're practically his wife, that boy better remember you."

"It's not his fault, Jade. The head injury caused him to have retrograde amnesia. Some stuff he's just not going to remember. I was praying I wasn't one of them."

"It's okay Morgan, he'll get better."

After talking to Jade for another twenty minutes, Morgan decided to give Dallas another try. Upon entering the room, he looked up and they made eye contact; he smiled and turned his attention back to the TV. Morgan walked in slowly, a little skeptical of his behavior. She decided she would just try to be his nurse before going back in.

"You feeling better, Mr. Streeter?" It would be easier than trying to make him remember her. Instead of answering, he looked straight ahead.

"Mr. Streeter, I asked how you're feeling. Nod yes if you're feeling fine, and shake your head no if you're not." She stopped in front of his bed. Once again, instead of doing what she had asked, he continued to stare at the television. "Well okay then, if you want to do it the hard way, then we will." She walked to the top of his bed and took his remote. She turned the TV off and put it on the windowsill. This got his attention, but only for a second. After looking at her for a moment, he turned his head and looked around the room.

Morgan looked at him with a hint of desperation in her eyes. "Dallas, do you feel like talking?"

After the surgery, it was important to observe his speech; they hadn't been able to get much more than a few words out of him all day. The few sentences he had with the doctor that performed his surgery earlier were enough to diagnose him and set his nurses up with a rehabilitation plan. Knowing him and how stubborn he was, she knew his rehabilitation was going to be a hard one if he continued this way.

While getting her degree, Morgan had interned at a rehab facility. The nurse she shadowed told her sometimes you would get patients that only responded if you were mean. She told Morgan this was because they responded better when they were being made to do something, versus given a choice. Although she hated to do it, if it made him better, she would be the mean nurse. She grabbed the bottom of his face and turned his head to her.

• • •

"Listen Dallas, you're going to have to talk to me whether you like it or not. I'd advise you to answer me when I speak to you." She stared him directly in the eyes.

Staring back at her, he frowned his face up and snatched away from her.

"I don't care about you being mad. If you would talk to me, then we could both do what we have to do and I could leave." Morgan stood back on her leg with her hands on her hips.

It was so hard for her to stand there and watch him be angry with her for nothing. She had to remember that until his memory started to return, he was her patient, not her man. Still not opening his mouth to say anything, Dallas shifted in the bed so that he was sitting on the side of it.

"I don't know what you think you're doing, because you can't walk on this leg until the swelling goes down." She strolled towards him and put his right leg back on the bed. He snatched away from her once he was secure on the bed.

"Don't touch me." His voice was low and raspy.

The hoarseness in his voice was an obvious sign he hadn't been talking in a few days. She was happy to hear it nonetheless. Morgan rolled her eyes at him.

"Trust and believe, I wouldn't touch you if I didn't have to." Inwardly, she wanted to laugh so hard.

His little attitude was funny. "Now back to my original question Mr. Attitude, how are you feeling?"

Dallas looked straight ahead at the blank television. "Fine."

"Good, do you need or want anything?" He said no without even looking at her. "Okay, well I'm leaving. Buzz the nurses' station if you change your mind." She exited his room.

"Girl, this boy has an attitude out of this world with me." Morgan laughed when Lay-Lay answered the phone.

Lay-Lay laughed with her. She asked Morgan why he had an attitude. All of them knew how stubborn Dallas could be. Morgan explained his condition to her and caught her up to speed. After she told her how he hadn't wanted her to touch him, they both laughed again.

"Well bitch, keep your hands to yourself." Lay was so happy to hear that Dallas was awake.

The only time Morgan's mood waivered was when she talked about him not remembering her. She said his temporary memory loss shouldn't last forever, but each person was different. Lay thought it was weird that he could only remember certain people based on when he'd met them. He couldn't remember anything that happened recently. The type of amnesia he had caused the recent happenings to fade. He would remember anything he'd known for a long time. When Lay-Lay heard this, the first thing she asked Morgan was what if he never remembered her? Morgan paused on the phone. That question was one Morgan had been avoiding in her mind since she read his charts. She had taken a moment to gather her feelings; she didn't want to cry again. She leaned over the nurse's station desk to look into his room. After watching him for a few seconds, she almost started crying again.

"Lay-Lay, I don't even know. I would say try to make him fall in love with me again, but it probably wouldn't even be the same."

That was the last thing she said before telling Lay she'd call her back. She had to keep busy before she let her thoughts get the best of her.

*****

Sitting in his car, D. Karter contemplated about going into the hospital. He had been sitting there for the last hour and a half trying to make up his mind. Going back and forth with the possibilities of what could happen, versus what would happen, was driving him crazy. When he first got the call, he was in Reno Valley, California with some of his connects making a drug deal. His right hand man had interrupted his meeting with the Columbian distributors to let him know there had been an emergency, and he needed to get to Atlanta as soon as he could. Wrapping up his meeting as fast as he could, he got on the first plane down South. He hadn't even stopped to drop his bags off.

He had went straight to the hospital from the airport. After lighting his blunt, he sat back in his seat and tried to ease his mind. The clock read **10:51,** so it was well after visiting hours. He tried reasoning with himself that Dallas' room should be empty by now. He really wasn't in the mood to run into anyone. He wanted to check on Dallas and leave. Blowing out another few rings of smoke, he put the blunt out and stuck it in the ash tray. *It's now or never,* he thought as he grabbed his hat and put it on his head. He pulled it down low over his eyes and walked into the hospital. He'd had everything checked out a few hours ago. Now he knew where Dallas was, so there was no need to waste time asking questions. He was almost to the top floor where Dallas was when the elevator stopped, and a nurse got on. She was a pretty little thing, definitely something he would have on his team. He looked her up and down, admiring the way her uniform fit her. He smiled when they made eye contact. She smiled and asked how he was doing.

"I'm fine. I'd be even better if I could get your name?" D. Karter was a smooth older man, tall with a broad build, deep dark skin, and a perfect smile. He wore his hair cut low with two parts right above his ear.

"I'm Morgan."

"That's a pretty name for a pretty lady," he smiled as the elevator stopped on the ICU floor. Morgan giggled lightly before saying thank you. He placed his hand at the small of her back.

"It was nice meeting you, Ms. Morgan. Hopefully I'll see you again before I leave."

Morgan gave a weak nod and exited the elevator. After he pressed the button waiting to be buzzed in the ICU unit, he watched Morgan retreat down the opposite hallway. He was going to make sure he saw her again. When the doors slid open, he looked for room 12. He had almost made it to the door when the nurse, Amber, stopped him.

"Sir visiting hours are over, only family can be here now."

"I am family, sweetheart," he smiled at her and kept walking. He possessed this commanding aura. He knew she wouldn't put up much of a fight. Instead, she just waved her hand and let him go on in. Morgan had told her to keep a strict eye on who went in and out. Since she'd let him in, she would watch him. She stood over the desk and spied through the glass. Dallas' room was completely dark except from the small lights from the various monitors he was hooked up to. Dallas was asleep, so D. Karter didn't say anything. He walked to the empty chair in the corner and sat down. He watched him for a long while. As he relaxed back in the chair, he watched Dallas' chest rise and fall.

He wanted to make sure Dallas' breathing was steady. He stirred a few times in sleep, but didn't wake up. Shaking his head, D. Karter ran a hand over his face and sighed. He missed his normal life. He missed being able to do normal things like watch his son sleep at night. The life he lived was a dangerous one, and he couldn't possibly subject Dallas to the same thing. He had left when Dallas was eight years old and hadn't been back since. Although he hadn't been in the house with him physically, he had been there every step of the way. From the time Dallas was child until now, he'd kept tabs on him at all times.

He knew every move Dallas made, and Dallas' wasn't even aware of it. There had been times he wanted to be with Dallas, but he didn't want to interrupt the life Marcy and Willie had given him; because of that, he kept his distance. When Dallas was born, it was the happiest day of his life. He enjoyed being a father more than anything. As time went on and he got more involved in the dope game, neither his freedom nor his life were guaranteed. There was no way he'd bring that type of heat on Marcy. and especially not Dallas, so he left. Although he sent Marcy a large check every month to make sure they were good, it didn't make up for him not being there. Standing, he walked over to the side of Dallas' bed so he could get a good look at him. Dallas looked exactly like him minus the color. He was dark whereas Dallas was more of a brown complexion, like his mother. Other than that, they were twins. D. Karter reached out and touched Dallas' hand lightly; he didn't touch him long, because he was too afraid to wake him. Satisfied, he removed his hand and went back to the chair. He stayed there watching him for another hour before he dozed off. He was so tired from his flight that he hadn't even noticed he was asleep until the nurse from the elevator woke him up. She was checking Dallas' vitals and IV fluids.

"Sir, you do know it's after visiting hours, right?"

D. Karter waited for a second allowing his eyes to focus. He looked up to see was Dallas still asleep before responding.

"Well aren't you a beautiful sight to wake up to."

Morgan shook her head and walked back up to the sides of Dallas' bed.

"What's going on with him?"

Morgan hesitated for a second before asking was he family. She made sure to tell him that they couldn't disclose Dallas' personal information to strangers. He understood her skepticism being that she didn't know who he was.

"Yeah, you can say that. I'm a friend of Marcy's."

She looked at him for a little bit longer before she began explaining what was going on with Dallas.

D. Karter shifted in the seat and leaned down, resting his elbows on his knees. "So they don't know who did it yet?"

"No sir, but they're working on it."

Nodding his head in understanding, he stood to leave. "Well I appreciate that, beautiful. I'll be back tomorrow night."

"Would you like me to tell him you stopped by?"

"Nah it's okay. I'll try to catch him tomorrow." After that, he exited Dallas' room.

*****

Arlington Taylor was the man to see. He had always succeeded in everything he put his mind to–from school to the marines. Now working for the CIA, he had always been the most hardworking and dedicated man to his obligations. Precision, loyalty, and intelligence were his core values. That was why he was about to get rid of one of his most recent recruits. Marley Woods was the newest member of the CIA task force, and she was proving to be very sloppy. He had brought her aboard a few months ago for this particular case as a favor for her uncle. He and her uncle had been working together for the past six years. He too was a little unsure of her emotional stability, and how it would affect her performance on the job, but chose to go ahead and give her a shot. Her uncle and Arlington both assumed this would be an easy beginning, being that she had history with the people and the city; unfortunately, she was doing a horrible job. Had Arlington known she would let her personal feelings get involved with her work, he would have picked someone else. The only reason he had yet to cut her loose was because she had one more task to complete; this would prove whether she was worth his time.   If she failed, she was fired. Just moments prior, he had spoken with her and she was emotional because one of the individuals involved in their current case wasn't doing too well. By no means was he cold hearted, but when there was work to be done, that came first. He had no sympathy for her, because this was her doing from the beginning. Now that he knew who the victim was, it was worse. He had given her an objective and a solution, and it was up to her to put it all together and make it work. Because she was in training, he wasn't able to give her any supporting ideas; now she was on the verge of screwing this all up.

"Do you think she can handle this?" Hannah referred to their only daughter.

"I know she can honey. Morgan is a smart girl, not to mention strong. She'll be fine. It's Marley I'm worried about. Once Morgan finds out about her, she's as good as dead."

Initially he hadn't wanted to be a part of this case, but once he found out his daughter was dating

Dallas, he changed his mind. He'd do anything for her. Morgan hadn't come right out and told her father everything that had gone on yet. When she called and asked for help, he knew it was on then. He had taught Kyle and Morgan everything he knew, and it definitely paid off. They were both strong, especially Morgan. Kyle was a great man and soldier, but he was caring and kind hearted like Hannah. Morgan was more head strong and ruthless like him. She was a true warrior, and that's what scared him. Morgan was fearless when it came to her loved ones. From what Kyle had told him when he was visiting, she was in love with Dallas. When he told Marley to come up with a plan to get D. Karter and Dallas in the same place, he didn't mean for her to practically kill the boy. She should have been able to come up with a better and less harmful plan.

"I think bringing Marley on was a mistake." Hannah massaged his shoulders as he spoke. "Arlington, maybe this case was just too personal for her first one."

"Hannah, this is a serious job. You can't pick and choose what cases you get and don't get. You just have to be prepared, and mentally ready for everything, and she isn't." He breathed hard again.

Hannah expressed her understanding before asking what he planned to do. He told her his baby, Morgan, had asked for help, and he would provide it. As far as Marley was concerned, she had just better work fast before Morgan caught on. Hannah kissed his cheek and left the room. Her husband was hopeless when it came to Morgan. When she saw him with his phone, she already knew he was talking to their daughter. A few moments later, her thoughts were confirmed when she heard him talking.

"Hey sweetheart, you busy?"

"Not too busy for my favorite guy. What you got for me?"

Arlington laughed at her and began explaining his findings. He'd found the recent hire roster, work schedules, and video surveillance of the hotel she'd given him. After rummaging through all of it, he had come up with the name Tasheena McCray. Morgan had no idea who she was. She hadn't recognized her that night, so her name really didn't ring a bell. Once he told her she was only nineteen, he asked Morgan what was her plan. He didn't want Morgan getting involved in anything that could get her into trouble.

"Don't worry Daddy, I'm not going to do anything major to her. I'm just going to beat her up for lying to me." They both shared a laugh before Arlington got serious again.

"After you beat her up, what do you plan on doing? If she tells you who it was, then what?"

That made her pause for a second. He knew her first thought was to kill them, but she didn't want to come right out and say it. She held the phone for another few minutes without saying anything. She was waiting for him to say what they were both thinking.

"Morgan, No. That's not your place. Find them and take it to the police. Do you understand me?"

She said yes sir to let him know she would do as he said. She respected her father and his judgment. If he didn't think this was right, then she would listen.

"That's my baby. How's your boyfriend?"

"He's fine, Daddy, but he has amnesia and he doesn't remember me."

He could hear in her voice that she was hurting. Although he hated it, there was nothing he could do for her. He told her it would all work itself out eventually if she kept her faith. He knew God would see Morgan and Dallas through this ordeal. Morgan held the phone a moment longer without speaking. Arlington knew it was something else. He asked her what was going on, and promised it would stay between the two of them. They were always keeping secrets from Hannah. When she made him promise not to be mad, he knew it was something serious.

"I'm kind of pregnant."

Arlington chuckled lightly. "Morgan there is no such thing as kind of pregnant. Either you are or you aren't, sweetheart."

When he asked her how far along she was, she told him thirteen weeks. Just before he could finish talking to her, Hannah walked back into his study.

"So this has been going on for about 3 months now, huh?" He was purposely being evasive. Morgan picked up on his change of voice, and asked was her mom nearby.

"Yes but it's okay. I'll handle it. Is that all you needed from me today?"

"There's one more thing, Daddy. I'm having twins."

"OH WOW MORGAN!" His response came out a little more excited than he'd meant it to. Now his wife had turned around and was looking at him. When Hannah asked what was going on, he lied saying Morgan was telling him about Dallas. He'd tell Hannah when Morgan was more comfortable with it. Morgan told him she loved him and would call him later. She was about to hang up when she heard him call her name.

"A picture of daddy's baby would be nice." She needed to send him an ultrasound photo; he desperately wanted to see the babies.

"Sure thing, but make sure you erase it. You know how nosey mommy can be."

He laughed and promised he would before they hung up.

Hearing that she was pregnant had knocked him off his feet, but he couldn't say he wasn't happy about it. He couldn't wait until the babies got there. Lying back in his chair, he went back to thinking about Marley and her position on his team.

Chapter 5

The next morning, Dallas lay awake in his hospital bed watching TV. He hated being in the hospital, but he still wasn't well enough to go home. He was getting better, but he was still in ICU. The doctors needed to monitor his brain activity. Although he had people coming and going, he still felt alone. His room was constantly filled with visitors, but he didn't recognize half of them. He was so sick of people trying to explain who they were when he couldn't remember them; it was beyond frustrating. His mom and dad had been there, and so had his cousin and best friend. Even his ex-girlfriend, Marley, had been there, but that was as far as he could remember. He used the railing on the side of his bed to sit up. A sharp pain ripped through his chest, causing him to cry out. Dallas winced in pain and sat back for a second to regroup before he tried again. His room door burst open before he could move.

In walked his nurse, claiming she'd heard him scream. She asked if he was okay, and he told her yes. His voice came out harsher than he'd meant for it to. She obviously didn't care about his attitude, because she continued asking questions. Once he told her he'd tried to sit up and it hurt, she explained why. The broken ribs he'd suffered from the attack hadn't completely healed yet. He would be in minor pain until they did. He blew her off with his face frowned up. His attitude had finally gotten to her, so she rolled her eyes and turned to leave.

His tone matched the disgusted look on his face. "Yo, what you rolling your eyes and shit for?"

"Because you have a nasty ass attitude, that's why." Morgan was looking at him like he was stupid.

"What the fuck kind of nurse are you talking to me like that?"

"The kind that's sick of your shit. Every time I come in here to check on your ass, you've, got a fucking attitude. When I leave you in here to kill your damn self you'll appreciate me. Now the next time you need something, don't buzz the nurses' station. Walk your crippled ass wherever you need to go and get it yourself." She said it with so much attitude he couldn't help but to laugh at her.

"You sure are a bitter ass nurse, with a filthy fucking mouth. You need to check that shit. If you was my woman, I would hem your little ass up so quick. You wouldn't dare spit no shit like that to me."

Morgan rolled her neck and smacked her lips. "First of all, with the attitude you have, I would never be your woman. Thank you very much."

Dallas couldn't do anything but smile. She was so pretty and small, just how he liked his women. He watched her every day coming in and out of his room. She was so attentive to him, and that's what pissed him off. He had never been the type to need anybody, but as of right now, he did. She was always popping in and out, bringing his food or sneaking him Gatorade. She even seemed to have formed a bond with his mom and friends, but he was still mean to her. He had to apologize to her after he got done thinking about his actions. He'd been angry at her all this time just for caring and doing her job. Dallas had been so mean to her that he hadn't even taken the time out to learn her name. He looked around her head and read her name off of the patient board in his room.

"Morgan, so you mean to tell me if I wasn't locked up in this hospital, you wouldn't give me any play?" The look on her face told him she was slightly taken back by what he had just said, so it took her a minute to respond.

"Boy no. You're too mean. I would be knocking your ass out every day."

He burst out into a laughter so infectious she had to laugh as well. He had to hold his stomach, he was laughing so hard.

"Check this out M, you really should stop cursing like that, it's not cute to hear that kind of shit coming out of a lady's mouth."

Morgan looked stunned for a minute; Dallas even thought he'd saw water in her eyes. Instead of responding, she looked towards the door so he wouldn't see her cry. *Damn what I say?* He didn't understand—one minute they were laughing, now she was about to cry. He asked her if she was okay. For some reason, he had this raging urge to comfort her, but his body wouldn't let him. The moment he saw her eyes water, he wanted to hold her in his arms. She could leave all of her troubles on him. Finally turning back around to face him, she smiled.

"Yeah Mr. Attitude, I'm fine. Don't try to be nice to me now." He laughed at her comment.

"I'm not. I just wanted to make sure you weren't bipolar or no shit like that. One minute we were laughing, and the next came the fucking waterworks. I just didn't understand."

"Oh shut up. I just got a lot going on right now, that's all."

"You want to talk to me about it? It's not like I got nothing better to do," Dallas held his arms out and playfully circled the room, showing her there was nothing else that had his attention.

He really didn't have anything better to do, but that wasn't the real reason he wanted her to talk to him. He was sincerely interested in why she was crying. He wanted to be there for her the same way she'd been there for him the past couple of days.

"Nah Dallas, I'm okay. I just had a moment. I'll be alright. I appreciate the thought, though. That's big coming from your mean ass."

Instead of saying anything, he just smiled at her. He liked the way she sounded when she laughed.

"What I just tell you about your mouth, girl?" He was going to stop her from cursing one way or the other. She told him she forgot and asked him did he need anything else.

*****

She needed to hurry and leave him; it was getting overwhelming. Having a normal conversation with him was getting to be too much. It was like she was talking to him, but she wasn't. He broke her from her thoughts, letting her know he didn't need anything. He also told her if she changed her mind about talking he'd be there. Morgan practically ran from the room. She needed some fresh air. Her emotions were all over the place. She thought she was going to faint when he'd called her M. That was the best thing she'd heard all day, aside from his laugh.

*****

A few hours later, Dallas had just woke up from a nap when King walked in. They dapped each other up before he sat down. He asked Dallas how he was feeling as he took his jacket off. Dallas let him know he was better than yesterday before joking on his clothes. He didn't know why King was dressed so corporate until King reminded him of his new job. It took King a minute to realize Dallas didn't remember anything that had just recently happened. He didn't even remember Jade.

He knew she was King's wife, but that was it. King had just finished telling him about their wedding day when Morgan walked in to change his medication. She spoke to King at the same time he asked her what time she got off. He told her Jade wanted her to come over and twist her hair. Morgan laughed at the confused look on King'   s face as he relayed the message. He had no idea about the hairstyle Jade was requesting. She and King went on for a few more minutes talking about Jade never answering her phone when Dallas interrupted them.

"Aye Nurse Attitude, don't come in here talking to my fam like you know him."

She rolled her eyes and licked her tongue at him. "Dallas shut up. You don't run me. All the time you've been in here not talking to me, they were. Now they're my friends too."

"Oh I don't run you Morgan?" His voice was laced with seduction.

"No sir you do not."

He smiled as he leaned forward, trying to sit up. He yelled out in pain again from his ribs. Her and King both ran to his bedside, trying to help him sit up. She asked him repeatedly was he all right as she watched him get himself back together.

"I told you I ran you." Judging by the unsteady smile on his face, he was obviously still in pain from moving. King sat back down, laughing at Dallas' prank. When she let him go, she slapped his shoulder.

"That was so stupid. Why would you do that? Who on Earth would purposely cause themselves excruciating pain just to prove a point? I should slap you upside your damn head." She walked away, clearly pissed about his little stunt. He held his chest as he laughed at her attitude.

"King, you're laughing too? Okay then, watch and see don't I tell Jade about y'all being so damn childish." Morgan rolled her eyes and grabbed some gloves.

King apologized as he tried to catch his breath from laughing.

"Whatever, don't neither one of y'all say anything else to me the whole time I'm in here." She began changing the IV needle in Dallas' arm.

"Bruh you haven't found out who did this yet?" Dallas instantly changed the mood back to a serious one. With no hesitation, King let Dallas in on the little information he had. He told him they had a name, but that was it. He left out the detail about Morgan being the one to give him that lead. He assured him that he'd let him know once he found out more. Dallas was happy to hear that, because he wanted payback. When it was time, he was seeking revenge on anybody that had something to do with his attack. Until then, he had to wait until he got better. Once they finished talking, King said he had to go, because tonight was he and Jade's date night.

"So Morgan, can I keep you company tonight, or is it date night for you too?"

"Yeah you can, even though my boyfriend might be mad." The face he made was hilarious.

Dallas tried to hide it, but he felt a tinge of jealousy. "Damn, you got a man?"

"Something like that."

Dallas asked her what kind of answer that was—either she did or she didn't.

"Well I had a boyfriend, but he left me for a while. Now I don't know if he's ever coming back. I don't want to count him completely out, because I know he loves me, but I don't want to hold on to false hope. I don't want to stay here thinking he's coming back and he never does."

Dallas could hear the sadness in her voice. The way her face dropped when she talked about her man, she was obviously in love with him. *Why would he leave her?* He wondered. He grabbed her hand and squeezed it.

"Damn, that's fucked up Morgan. You all right?"

She told him yeah as she tried to smile. He could tell she was faking her smile, but he didn't want to push, so he changed the subject.

"I like your hair. It looks really nice." He reached up to touch it. It was so soft.

"Thank you, I just got it done this morning."

"Well it looks good." He let her hand go and turned the TV on.

Once she finished what she was doing, she grabbed everything and left. Dallas leaned back on his pillow and thought about his life. He wished he had a woman to love him, someone to be there with him right now making sure he was recovering properly. It would be nice to have somebody that missed spending time with him outside of the hospital. The closest thing he had to that was his nurse, and that was making him feel pathetic. When he looked out of the glass door, he saw Morgan talking to his other nurse Amber.

She was so pretty, and he loved her personality. He couldn't believe how mean he had been to her before. He didn't know what kind of man she was involved with that would just leave her. All he could think about was how he would never do that. She seemed like the perfect catch. He didn't understand what man in his right mind would just pick up and vacation, while knowing she was at home waiting for him. Before he could turn his head, she turned around and caught him staring. She smiled and waved; he nodded his head at her and turned his attention back to the TV. A little while later, she stuck her head back into his room letting him know she would be leaving for a little while. She asked if he needed anything, and he declined.

"You sure? Not even a snicker, or some teriyaki beef jerky?" His head snapped around instantly.

"Yes please."

She smiled and closed the door back.

After she left, he wondered for a minute how she could have known that he liked those things. *Maybe my mom told her.*

*****

It had only been three hours since she left the hospital and Morgan was already ready to get back. She wasn't used to being away from Dallas that long. She missed him, so she packed a bag and headed back to the hospital. Once she got on his floor, she started to get nervous. What if he didn't want to see her? Figuring she had nothing to lose, she knocked on his door and entered.

"What's up Pretty girl? What are you doing here? I thought you were off for the rest of the night?"

"I am. I was bored at home by myself, so I figured I'd come spend some time with my favorite patient."

The way he blushed was the cutest. She missed him so much. She took her bag off and placed it in the chair. When he asked why she had a bag, and she told him just in case she spent the night, he laughed. She was almost embarrassed as he continued to make fun of her for being lonely.

"I'm just kidding. I've got plenty of room in my bed, you can sleep in here with me."

She smiled, because he had no idea that was exactly what she had planned on doing from the beginning. He didn't know that though, so she played it cool.

"I can't be sleeping in here with you. I have a man, and the nurses be in and out all night. I wouldn't get any sleep."

Dallas grabbed her arm and pulled her onto the bed. "Honestly Morgan, the nurses wouldn't be the reason you wouldn't get any sleep." He leaned closer to her and inhaled her scent. She pushed his head away and scooted back some. "Forgive me if I'm over stepping my boundaries, but you need to be taking applications for a new man as well. Considering yours just up and left you, no offense."

"You are so nasty. While you're playing, who said I would even give you the time of day?"

"Nobody has to tell me. I can tell myself. I've been seeing you checking your boy out when I'm at physical therapy and shit."

She laughed, unable to play it off. She had been watching him for the past few days at physical therapy. It eased her mind when she could see him making progress. Dallas pulled her to the top of the bed next to him.

"Come lay down with me, M."

Before lying down, she locked his room door, pulled the curtains closed, and took her pants off. Morgan got into the small bed with him. She'd already told the nurses on duty she was staying with him, that way they wouldn't come in at odd hours of the night. Working at the hospital had its benefits. She was so glad they had moved him from ICU earlier that day, and he was now in his own room.

Dallas watched Morgan with pure lust. She looked cute in her panties and Clark Atlanta T-shirt. After pulling her vent brush from her bag, she stood on her knees in the bed so she could see the mirror above his sink and wrapped her hair. Once she was finished, she tied her scarf around her head. Dallas made jokes about her scarf, but Morgan didn't care. She didn't play about her hair. When she was sure her scarf was on tight enough, she snuggled under the blanket with him. Dallas grabbed his remote from the side of the bed and turned the TV off. Once he turned the lights above his bed off, the room was black dark.

"Is it okay if I touch you, Morgan?" He sounded a little nervous.

Morgan nodded her head yes, but playfully told him not to feel on her, even though that was exactly what she wanted. He placed his hand on her thigh and ran it up her leg until he stopped at her waist. He used his good arm to pull her backwards into him. His whispers in her ear about how right she felt in his arms had her feeling vanquished with emotion. When she agreed to lay with him, she was surprised the smile on his face didn't light up the room. They lay there in the dark holding each other for a few minutes before either of them said anything. Dallas flipped over onto his back and pulled Morgan up to sit on him.

"Turn around and get up here, M."

Since Morgan was now straddling him, she had to sit still for a minute to readjust her eyes to the darkness. While she tried to focus, Dallas rubbed his hands all over her body. From her butt to her breasts, Dallas was feeling her up like a mad man. He paused for a moment to ask was she all right. He apologized if he was offending her with his forwardness. She said it was okay, but he still felt the need to explain himself. He kept telling her that although they had grown pretty close since he'd been at the hospital, he didn't want to make their friendship awkward. She dismissed him immediately. After his hands probed her body a little more, he stopped. He laid back and rested his arms behind his head. He asked her to tell him about herself. She felt weird having this conversation with him being that he already knew everything about her, but she answered anyway. They stayed up half the night laughing and talking. Morgan couldn't have been happier.

*****

Rummaging through her closet looking for her computer charger, Marley didn't even hear her cell phone ringing. Even if she had, she probably still wouldn't have answered it. She was so stressed over finishing up this case with Dallas and D. Karter. Everything seemed to be a pretty easy take down in the beginning, but that was proving to be very difficult. Whenever she thought she had everything figured out, something else would come up. She had been wanting to get back up to the hospital to sit with Dallas, but that wasn't happening. Morgan was always there and acting suspicious of her. Although Morgan had every reason to be suspicious, she still didn't want to come off as nervous, so she tried to avoid her.

Her phone began ringing again. This time she grabbed it off the bed and answered it. She said hello a tad bit more annoyed than intended. It was Neko, and she didn't really want to be bothered. He made small talk asking what she was doing for the day. She didn't necessarily want to spend any time with him, but he was her cover up. Maybe talking to him would even take her mind off of everything else she had going on. He invited her to dinner and a movie later that evening. They finalized their plans and ended the call.

Marley lay on her bed staring at the ceiling for a little while before deciding to go see Dallas. She got up, grabbed her purse, and left her house. By the time she reached the hospital, it was a little after six and his room was packed with visitors. They had moved him to a regular room earlier that week, and his family was taking full advantage of the new visitation rules. Entering the room, she noticed his parents in the corner by his bed. King and Smoke were leaning against the windowsill, and Jade and Lay-Lay were in the two chairs against the wall. Along the other wall were two massive sized men with Men of Steel shirts on talking to Dallas. Everyone's eyes looked up to see who had just come in the door. They all said their greetings before going back to what they were doing, all except Marcy. She came over to make sure it was her. She wore a large smile as she asked her how she'd been. They hugged as Marley asked her the same. After she told her she was fine now that Dallas was better, she grabbed her hand and led her up the side of the bed. Dallas nodded as she came around the corner. She asked how he was feeling as he drank from the Gatorade bottle in his hand. He was just about to answer when he was interrupted.

*****

"Hey Marley." Lay-Lay's tone overflowed with sarcasm.

Marley waved and turned back around. Jade burst out laughing at how messy Lay-Lay was being.

"Lay-Lay you're so stupid." Her and Jade were talking and laughing only loud enough for the two of them to hear.

"Girl I just wanted her to see us before she started getting too friendly. I would hate to slap her in this hospital. I already owe her ass a beat down."

Marley turned her attention back to Dallas. It was easy to tell she was trying her hardest to focus on Dallas, but Lay-Lay kept saying slick stuff loud enough for her to hear. Lay-Lay heard Marley trying to encourage him about his rehabilitation process, but he didn't seem very optimistic. Marley even placed her hand on his arm as a reassuring gesture.   Across the room, Jade and Lay-Lay were watching her every move. Lay wasn't feeling how touchy Marley was being. When she noticed her hand on him, she rolled her eyes. Marley having left it there a minute too long for her liking, Lay-Lay got up, picked her hand up off of Dallas' arm, and dropped it dramatically. Lay-Lay got into her space for a quick second, daring her to say anything before retreating back to her seat. She gave Marley a knowing look.

"Act like you know."

Marley sucked her teeth. "Act like I know what Lay-Lay?"

Glad that Dallas' mom and dad had just walked out to get him some food, Lay-Lay stared at her.

"Act like you know he ain't yours, bitch."

"Oh here we go." Marley released an exasperated sigh.

Lay-Lay stood up and walked closer to Marley. She had absolutely no problem correcting whatever attitude problem Marley thought she had.

"Yeah little bitch, here we fucking go."

"Look honey, to be for real, right now he isn't either one of ours." Marley crossed her arms across her chest just as Lay-Lay drew her hand back. Smoke had to grab it to keep her from slapping Marley. After looking around the room, Dallas asked them what was the issue. Clearly he was unaware of the ongoing beef between the two ladies.

"There isn't a problem. This hoe just needs to learn her place and stay there," Jade answered for them.

King rubbed Jade's arm, willing her to calm down. Right then wasn't the time or the place. Looking between the two women and then up to King and Smoke, Dallas just shook his head. He didn't know what the problem was, but he was too exhausted to even ask. Marley had just grabbed her purse and let Dallas know she'd come back at another time when his room door opened. In walked Morgan—it was definitely time for her to go now. She spoke to everyone in the room as she came around the corner. Jade got up to hug Morgan.

"Hey boo. It's about time you got here."

"Y'all know I have an appointment today, so I had to get dressed. This is my first day off in three weeks."

Dallas smiled at Morgan. She was dressed casually in light gray joggers and a black fitted shirt. This was the first time he'd seen her in something other than her scrubs she wore every day. She looked even more beautiful with her hair curled loosely on the long side and in the front by her bangs. The big gold earrings she wore matched perfectly with the small gold necklace around her neck. He had it bad for this nurse, but she had a man. He'd never been the type to step on another man's toes. Although Dallas was thinking it, Lay-Lay said it. Morgan smiled when she told her how pretty she looked.

"You know I had to get cute for my date."

She had an ultrasound appointment in another hour on the OB floor of the hospital. She was extremely excited; Jade and Lay-Lay were too.

"Would it be tacky if we tagged along on your date?" Before Morgan could answer Jade, Dallas interrupted her.

"Who are you going on a date with, M? Your man came back?"

She smiled and shook her head no. For some reason, she felt nervous around him, but she didn't know why. After all, he was and had been her man for a while now. Furthermore, she had just spent the night with him a few hours ago. Morgan turned back to her two best friends and told them she was hoping they would come with her. Of course, they were overjoyed.

"Well Dallas, like I said, I'll come back later when your room is less crowded." Marley purposely drew attention to herself.

As if just noticing Marley was even in the room Morgan rolled her eyes. "What are you doing here?"

"I came to check on Dallas. I didn't know he had all of these visitors, or I would have waited."

Morgan knew Marley was full of it. Something in the back of her mind told her Marley had something to do with this whole ordeal, she just didn't know what.

Morgan walked closer to Marely. "Oh no. Please don't mind us. After all, you are the reason he's alive." A sinister smile adorned her face.

"Word? Marley, you're the one that found me?" Dallas' voice was hyped with enthusiasm.

"Uh yeah D, but it's no big deal." Marley shifted uncomfortably.

He grabbed her hand. "The hell it ain't. I owe you my life."

Watching Dallas get all sweet on Marley made Morgan's blood boil, but she remained calm.

"Oh yeah. Marley, I'm glad you're here. I've been meaning to talk to you about that anyway. What did the two men look like? I'm trying to find them." All eyes went to King.

Jade leaned against him and smiled. She and her friends were all glad he'd put Marley on the spot. She had to bite her bottom lip to keep from kissing him right then; King was low-key being messy. Morgan realized what he was doing and laughed on the inside. Men were just like females. Now that all eyes had shifted back to her, she couldn't stand the heat. She told King they had on ski masks and she didn't see their faces. King nodded his head and remained quiet. After that, she bid Dallas goodbye and left.

Chapter 6

Once the room was clear of any extra company, everyone relaxed.

"Has anybody been in here to change the bandage on his head yet?" Morgan was talking to no one in particular, but was answered by Smoke. He had been there since he'd gotten off work that morning.

"Not since earlier."

Morgan placed on a pair of gloves and grabbed some stuff to change his bandage. When she walked closer to him, Dallas was able to smell her perfume. It was intoxicating. The smell triggered something in his brain. His mind wondered to a day when he was at a motorcycle function. He was hugging a woman. The memory was vague, but he knew it had to be real. He could see pretty much the entire scene in his mind. He sniffed a little harder as she leaned over him to rewrap the bandage. He tried to see if he could remember anything else, a face of the woman or something, but he couldn't. That was it. When he looked up, he was eye level with her breasts. Morgan was so close he could read the initials **MS** on her necklace. He didn't know why he was about to do it, but he asked anyway.

"Morgan, do you ride motorcycles?"

That got everybody in the room's attention. The only people that remained were his close friends. His parents and coworkers had left a while ago. Morgan stepped back so she could make eye contact with him before she answered.

"Yeah. Why you ask me that?"

"When you leaned over me, I could smell your perfume. It made me think about this time I was at some motorcycle thing, hugging a girl."

"Did you recognize the girl?" Eagerness took over her every word.

"No. I couldn't see her face. I just remember hugging her tight, and smelling that perfume. The visuals were really vague." His eyebrows scrunched up.

He looked defeated that he couldn't remember a face. He looked at Morgan for some answers as to why his memories were like that, but she looked just as disturbed as he did.

"Yeah I ride motorcycles. I actually rode mine here today. I could take you downstairs to look at it if you want."

"Nah that's okay. My head is hurting a little. I think I just need to go to sleep." Dallas laid back and closed his eyes.

It was so frustrating not being able to remember stuff. He could tell by the looks on all of his friends faces that there was more to the motorcycle story. It almost angered him that they hadn't said anything. His memory was getting better day by day, but still foggy in certain areas. He was remembering a variety of things as time passed. Today when he saw his friends from work in their uniforms, it brought back the memory of his business and how he had started it. In his mind, he wanted to believe the girl at the race track in his memory was Morgan, but how could that be when she was his nurse? His mom had told him she was his friend, but he was sure if she was more than that, his mom would have told him.

He was starting to think he was becoming infatuated with her. Morgan was constantly on his mind. When she wasn't working, he wondered where she was. He even found himself trying to make conversation when she would come to check on him, just so she would stay longer. His thoughts were interrupted by a small voice asking if he was okay. It was Morgan. Once he opened his eyes, he noticed that everyone had cleared the room, and no one remained but the two of them.

"I'm good. I just can't stand only being able to remember bits and pieces of my life."

Morgan sat down on the bed next to him and leaned her head on his shoulder.

"Don't get discouraged, Dallas. Recovery takes time; you're doing very well."

"Thanks Morgan, but I want to do better. I want to know what's going on around me. I want to know why I feel so attached to you." The latter part of his sentence was a little quieter than the rest. He really didn't understand.

"Trust me Dallas, I understand the lost feeling you have right now. You probably feel close to me because I've been your constant nurse. I'm always around doing pretty much everything a girlfriend would do. I think that's why."

He thought about what she said and decided not to respond. Morgan laid there a few more minutes before she got up and fixed her clothes. She told him she had to go, but would stop back by on her way home.

"Who are you going on a date with?" Dallas hadn't wanted to ask, because it was none of his business, but he had to know.

"There's two special people in my life right now. I have to check on them periodically, it's not a real date." Her smile eased his mind.

Just as she was about to walk out, he called her name.

"What's your whole name?"

She held the door handle, with one foot out of the door. "Morgan Taylor."

"What's your middle name?"

"It's Domonique. Why?"

"I know it's none of my business, but I was trying to figure out what the **MS** on your necklace stood for."

Morgan looked like she was debating in her head whether or not to say anything. He wasn't sure why, so he was prepared to dismiss the question entirely until she began talking again.

"It stands for Morgan Streeter."

She stayed there for a moment looking for any signs of realization, but there was none, so she left. When Morgan said his last name, his mind went all over the place. He knew now deep down inside she must have meant something to him before. This would explain the crazy attachment he felt to her. He let out an angry yell as he hit the side of his bed. He wanted to remember her. He needed to feel some love. Dallas desired to feel compassion from a woman other than his mother. He could tell the way she interacted with all of his peoples that they had known each other long before he got into the hospital. He just couldn't significantly place her. After picking up his phone, he called the one person he knew would tell him anything he wanted to know. She answered on the first ring.

"Hey Mama, what are you doing?"

"Nothing baby. I just got done cleaning your house. How are you feeling?"

"Frustrated. I need you to help me remember, Ma. I hate feeling like this." Dallas did something he hadn't done in a long time–cry.

Listening to her son cry tore Marcy's heart up. The doctors told her he had a long road to recovery and it would be a hard one, but she wanted to help any way she could. The therapist told her to try not to say too much, but there was no way she was going to sit here and listen to her son cry, especially when she could help him.

"What do you want to know, baby?" Marcy sat down on the couch. She was prepared to fill in whatever blanks the best she could.

After being on the phone with his mom for almost an hour and a half, Dallas felt better. Things made a little more sense than they had before. He didn't remember everything just yet, but with the new information he'd obtained from his mom, it was safe to piece things together. Dallas leaned over his bed and grabbed his walker. Once he finished using the restroom, he grabbed the photo album his mom had put together and sat on his bed. He was supposed to go over it that morning in rehab, but he had chosen not to. He was too afraid of what he might see. Pausing a moment before he opened it, he looked around the room for his cell phone. His mom had brought that along with the photo album. The album was a compilation of the most recent events in his life. Those were the only things he didn't remember. The first page of the book was a Men of Steel logo with pictures of his building and employees. It was obviously from the grand opening cookout. The next pages contained pictures of him, King, and Smoke on different occasions. Some pictures were of them at the club, basketball court, and around the house. Continuing to flip, he noticed a picture of him leaning next to a woman in a wedding dress. It was Jade, King's wife. He had been at their wedding. He smiled because he recognized them, and he vaguely remembered the wedding.   He continued to look. As he flipped through the book, he began remembering certain people and certain things, which motivated him to finish. When he turned the next page, he stopped; his breath had gotten caught in his chest. It was a picture of him at the strip club with his friends. Everyone was in it—King, Jade, Smoke, Lay-Lay, and his nurse, Morgan. He was standing behind her with his arms wrapped around her waist, kissing her cheek. She had her arms circled around his, with her head leaning to the side from his kiss. He could tell just by looking at the picture that they were happy. His mom had told him they had only been dating a few months, but he was very fond of her. She explained to him how he hadn't been serious with anyone since Marley until he met Morgan. On the last two pages, he saw at least nine or ten more pictures of him and her. Some were of her alone, and some were of them together. One picture that stood out to him the most was them standing in front of the civic center. She was in a black cap and gown, holding her degree.

She had obviously just graduated from college, but that wasn't the part that caught his eye. It was the large banner that Smoke and Lay-Lay were holding. It read **Congratulations Nurse Taylor.** He looked at the picture for a little while longer before he decided that was enough for one day and closed the book. He pushed his cell phone across the bed with the album and chose to save that for another day. He thought he had wanted to know everything, but now he wished he didn't. It was easier for everyone to be strangers than for him to have relationships with people he couldn't remember.

"God, I just want to remember." His loud voice echoed off of the walls.

As he closed his eyes, he heard two knocks on his door, and in walked Morgan. He moved the pillow so she could sit down.

"How did your date go?" Morgan's smile was the biggest he'd ever seen. "Well I take it that it went well." Judging by her reaction, it had obviously gone fine.

"Yes, it was wonderful. I can't wait until the next time."

A little jealous of her reaction, Dallas turned his attention back to the passing cars outside his window. He was torn between wanting to know the truth, and feeling tortured that he couldn't remember any of it.

"What's on your mind, Dallas?"

Her face showed genuine concern, but he wasn't really in the mood for serious heart to hearts right now.

"Nothing, I just wish I could take a shower instead of these fucking sink baths."

After letting out the cutest giggle he had ever heard, Morgan got up off the bed and sat her purse on the table. She turned back towards him and told her they'd try to make that happen. He was unsure of how they were going to do that being that he could barely walk on his injured leg. There was no way he could stand in a shower by himself.

"I can help you. That's if you don't mind."

Dallas let a devious grin cross his face.

"So what exactly does you helping me consist of? Are you going to walk me in the bathroom and sit on the toilet until I finish? Or are you going to get in there and bathe me yourself to make sure I don't fall?"

"First of all, there's nothing wrong with your arms, so you can bathe yourself. Secondly. I'm only there as support to make sure you don't slip and bust your head."

"Okay. I'm forewarning you, a nigga is packing, so don't be drooling all over my dick when I take these shorts off." He smiled and she blushed.

Morgan knew firsthand what he was packing and was missing it like crazy. He didn't have to forewarn her of anything.

"Okay sir, I'll try not to do that." Her voice leaked with mockery.

After pushing his walker to him, she went into the bathroom and turned on his shower. By the time she was back in the room, he had taken off his hospital gown and was standing up waiting for her. She instructed him to walk into the restroom, and she'd help him remove his shorts and underwear. His leg had gotten a lot better since the first day he got there, but it was still sore, so he walked with a slight limp. With both of them in the bathroom, it felt a lot smaller.

She reached for his shorts.

"Okay are you ready?"

"No my dear, I think the question should be, are you ready?"

She laughed at him as she went to pull down his shorts and underwear, but there were none. Morgan scrunched her face up.

"Boy you are so nasty. You don't even have any underwear on."

"My dick is too big. They get uncomfortable."

Morgan couldn't take Dallas and his foolishness right then. She shook her head and proceeded to remove his garments. When he was completely nude, she slid the shower curtain back all the way so he could push the walker in with him. She had just gotten her hair done and didn't want the water and steam to mess it up.

● ● ●

She thought about it for a minute, but there was no other way to help him. Once she lathered up his washcloth, she handed it to him.

"You bathe everything you can, and whatever you can't do, I'll finish for you."

He bathed the upper part of his body with caution because, his ribs and abdomen were still a little sore. He washed his stomach and arms the best he could, then stopped when it was time to wash his private parts. He smiled and handed her the washcloth.

"I need help with everything else."

Morgan reached for his genitals without a second thought. She'd done it a million times before.

"I knew your nasty butt was going to do this. You could have bathed this mess yourself." Honestly, she was happy he was faking. She missed him. She was so exultant to be sharing something that intimate with him.

"Why it got to be mess though? I really did need your help. I can't be lifting nothing this heavy right now, my wrist is still fucked up." Dallas laughed at his own joke as he leaned his head against the wall.

He looked down and watched her movements as she continued cleaning him. By the time she was finished washing his legs and feet, she lifted her head and came face-to-face with the part of him that she missed the most. For a moment, she just stared at it. She was trying to decide whether or not to kiss the head or to try to remain professional. By the way it was starting to get stiff, she could tell Dallas was thinking the same thing. Looking up at him from her position on the floor, she could see the lust written all over his face. His breathing had picked up, and she could feel the heat radiating off of his skin.

"Umm...I think we're finished now." Morgan fought against the temptation and stood to her feet.

"Nah baby, I don't think we are." Dallas grabbed her by her waist and pulled her to him.

Their faces were only inches apart. When she told him that this was a bad idea, he pulled her closer, and tightened his grip around her. He was going to show her just how bad. Dallas' lips were so close to hers if she licked her tongue out, she would touch them. She was now completely inside the shower with him. Water was running all over her back and hair, but at that moment, she couldn't have cared less. Unable to put together one coherent thought, she lunged forward and kissed his lips with a hunger so intense she felt a little crazed. They kissed each other with so much desire and fervor it felt impossible to let go, but Morgan did—she had to. She tried to back out of the shower, but he locked his arms around her back to hold her in place.

"Please don't go." His tone was desperate "Please stay. I need you to stay."

Resting his forehead on the top of her shoulder, he tightened his grip around her waist and squeezed her to him. It was like he couldn't hold her close enough. He kept squeezing her closer, but it wasn't enough. It was in that moment she knew, whether he ever remembered her or not, she would never leave his side. They would just have to fall in love all over again. She would do anything but separate from him. She rested her head against his chest.

"I'm here, Dallas. I promise you, I'll never leave."

After another ten minutes of standing in the shower, they were finally out and back inside his room. Morgan had stripped from her wet clothing and changed into a pair of scrubs. Amber had brought them to her from her work locker. Her hair had curled up, leaving her no choice but to brush it up into a bun on the top of her head. She felt a mess, but to Dallas she still looked as beautiful as she always did. Once she was all put back together, she grabbed his things to help him get dressed. Because his ribs were still sore, he wore the hospital gown as a shirt. She draped the hospital gown back over him and helped him on the bed after pulling up his shorts. He thanked her, but she kept telling him there was no need.

"No, I mean for everything. I don't think I could have gotten this far without you being here."

She smiled to avoid the seriousness of the conversation.

"It's really no problem Dallas. That's what I'm here for."

For a long while, the room was filled with an awkward silence. She grabbed her things and announced she was leaving.

"Will I see you tomorrow?"

"Yep, I'm off for the rest of the night, but I'll come by and check on you in the morning." Morgan was just about to leave when she remembered she'd brought him something.

She pulled out a bag of unwrapped snicker mini's and tossed them on the bed with another blue PowerAde. His face lit up at the sight of the candy; he had been wanting another snicker all day, but kept forgetting to ask for one.

"Good looking out, M." He snatched the bag of candy off the bed.

"No problem. I'll see you later." She exited the room.

Dallas lie back smiling as he thought back on the shower he had just taken. It was hands down the best one he ever had, or at least the best one he could remember.

Chapter 7

Morgan pulled her phone out and called to let Jade know she was on her way over. When Jade told her she was getting dressed, Morgan hung up her phone and dropped it into her backpack. Once her helmet was on her head, she cranked her bike up and left the parking lot. Tonight her, Jade, and Lay-Lay were going to pay Miss Tasheena a visit. It had been on her to check the girl out since she'd gotten the info from her dad, but she hadn't had a break from the hospital up until today. It took her half an hour to get dressed and get back to Jade's house. She decided to drive her jeep tonight instead of her bike so they could all ride together. Before she could knock on the door, Lay-Lay came out.

"What's up little ugly girl."

Morgan sighed as she walked past Lay-Lay and into the house. "Tired and sexually frustrated. If Dallas doesn't hurry and get himself together, I'ma mess around and fuck his crippled ass."

"I don't even blame you girl. I've been miserable as hell. Being on oovoo with your fine ass brother doesn't make it any better." Morgan frowned her face up in disgust at Lay-Lay.

"Eww what the hell y'all be doing on oovoo?"

"Nothing. Kyle's ass don't be trying to do one thing."

Jade walked into her living room and butted into their conversation. "Lay, you're too nasty for your own good."

"Ain't she though? This chick is trying to talk about my brother because he got tact. Bitch don't be trying to turn my brother out."

Lay-Lay burst out laughing. "Just wait on it, my nigga."

Jade asked if they were ready after she kissed King's lips when he walked into the living room. He told them to be safe, and to call him if anything went wrong. They left out and headed on their way. When they got there, Morgan parked two houses down and killed her engine. Morgan told them that her dad had already scoped the place out and no one should be there but her right now. She lived with her dad and brother, but they were both at work. Once they'd loaded their guns, they exited the vehicle. All three women were armed, but didn't plan on using the guns unless they had to. Morgan knocked on the door. It took a minute for someone to answer it, but when she finally did, Morgan didn't give her a chance to say anything before she forced her way into the house. Tasheena stumbled backwards, tripped over her cat, and fell on the couch. She placed her hands in the air in surrender.

"I'm sorry, I don't know anything, please don't hurt me."

● ● ●

"We're not going to hurt you unless you continue to lie." Morgan moved in front of her.

The girl nodded her head and scooted to the edge of the sofa. When Morgan asked her who Dallas' attackers were again, she lied. This pissed Morgan off, because she'd just told her to stop lying. She pulled her gun from the waistband of her pants and pointed it at Tasheena's chest.

"Lie to me again, and I will blow your heart all over your daddy's white sofa."

She was crying harder now. Her eyes shifted side-to-side while she debated on giving them an answer. Morgan cocked her gun just for emphasis.

"It was a boy named Antoine Noble. I know him from around the way, he said him and his homeboy wanted to rob this nigga they knew, and asked me would I cut the cameras."

Jade walked in front of her. "So you don't know who the other boy was?"

She kept her eyes trained on Morgan's gun and shook her head no. Having the gun pointed at her brought back painful memories.

"I never saw him. Antoine came alone. The only reason I knew it was two of them was because he said it. I never actually saw the second person."

Morgan felt like she was telling the truth, but that didn't stop her from being mad. She lowered her gun and slapped the taste out of Tasheena's mouth. She told her she'd gotten slapped for not telling the truth in the beginning. Tasheena held her face and cried harder. She tried explaining to Morgan that they told her they'd kill her if she told, but Morgan didn't care. She just wanted answers. She wanted to know where she could find Antoine.

"He lives on Howard Street, down by the rec center. In some brown apartments. He lives with his baby mama in apartment C." She rambled off.

"Baby girl, I don't know why you keep looking over there at that door. You're not going anywhere any time soon." Morgan snatched her off of the couch and punched her in the face.

She was about to give her a taste of what her friends gave Dallas. Morgan wanted to take all of her anger out on Tasheena, but she stopped. She wasn't really putting up a fight. Hearing a car pull up, Lay-Lay went to the front door and looked out the window.
"Morgan it's a white pick up outside. I think it might be her daddy."

"That's okay. We're done here anyway." She turned around and grabbed her gun off the table.

"Please don't hurt my dad," Tasheena pleaded. Jade sucked her teeth at Tasheena's remark.

"Girl shut up. We aren't about to do anything to your lil daddy."

They opened the door and passed him coming in as they went out. Before they could make it down the side walk, he was back out the door with his shotgun. He was yelling about what they'd done to his daughter. As if on one cue, all three girls turned around with their guns aimed at the man. Lay-Lay spoke for the trio.

"Sir take your old ass back in the house."

As he looked down the barrels of six guns, he realized he didn't have a chance, so he scurried back inside. The girls got back into the truck and into their seatbelts. They took a moment to relax before talking. Morgan asked them did they want to go looking for Antoine. Lay-Lay wanted to, but Jade didn't.

"Y'all two hoes must have forgotten I'm a fed now? I can't be busting down people's doors," Jade reminded them. Morgan was a little confrontational, because she wanted to do it right then, but Jade came up with a better idea.

"How about I get Zion and KB to get him, and then we'll handle it like that? You don't need to be getting caught up in no mess either, Morgan."

She agreed and they left.

*****

It had been two weeks since Morgan beat up on Tasheena, and KB and Zion still hadn't been able to catch up with the boy Antoine. She knew she was going to have to find another way to do this. She had asked around a few of the right places, and found out his main hangout spots. She would make her move soon, but until then, she was at Emory working. She stopped in the food court downstairs, grabbed a salad from Chick-fil-A and a bottle of water, and headed to the elevator. Being pregnant with twins was no joke; she was constantly hungry and sore.

The further along she got, the bigger her bottom got. She had always had a little bit of butt to be her size, but she had gone from a size three in pants to a seven. Even though she couldn't fit any of her clothes, she couldn't pretend she wasn't enjoying it. Her stomach wasn't that big yet, but it was starting to poke out. You couldn't see it that well in her scrubs, but when she wore her regular tops it was plain as day. She was so busy texting Lay-Lay that when she stepped off the elevator, she bumped head first into the man standing in front of her. She started apologizing before she even saw the face of the person she'd hit. The moment they met eyes, her reaction changed.

"Well hello there beautiful." D. Karter's voice was very deep.

Morgan shifted her water in the crook of her arm. "Hi how are you? I haven't seen you in a few days."

D. Karter had been one of Dallas' frequent visitors, but only at night. Every time he came, Dallas would be asleep. Morgan assumed that's how he liked it, so she left him to it.

"I had to go out of town to handle some business, did you miss me?" His smile was bright.

He had one of the most gorgeous smiles she had ever seen. The only smile that looked better than his was Dallas'. *Ah shit!* After taking a moment to think about it, Dallas kind of favored this man. Better yet, he was the spitting image of him, minus the skin color. She smiled and continued to observe his features. How could she not have noticed this before? Dallas was this man's twin. Morgan barely heard anything else he said. She was too busy thinking about her recent findings. He said something again, but she had started walking away by now. Her mind was running a mile a minute. Now she knew why he came late at night when no one else was there. He probably didn't want to be seen. This was major a discovery for her, because as far as Dallas knew, his father was dead. He hadn't seen nor heard from him since he was eight. Morgan decided to keep this little secret to herself for now. She knocked on Dallas' room door. It was her lunch break, and she hadn't had as much time to spend with him in a few days because of her other patients, so she decided to eat in there. When she walked in, he was nowhere in sight. She sat her food down and was just about to go look for him when his bathroom door opened. He walked up behind her.

"Hey beautiful."

"What's up boy? Look at you walking without help."

His leg had gotten a hundred percent better, and although he still limped a little, he was able to walk without assistance. He had just told her his doctor was thinking about releasing him when she sat down and opened her food.

"I'm kind of excited, but then again I'm kind of not."

"Why wouldn't you be happy? It's been almost two months that you've been here. You should be running out the door." Morgan filled her mouth with salad.

"I'm happy as hell to be going home, but that means I won't be able to see you every day."

Dallas still hadn't gained his full memory back, but it was a lot better. Even though he didn't remember their past relationship, they had formed a totally different bond since he'd been there. Morgan knew what they were to each other, and so did he to an extent. She tried to make him feel better by telling him she'd come see him at physical therapy, but even she knew that wasn't the same.

"I like how we kick it every day. I look forward to you coming in here to be honest with you."

"How about I give you my number, and we can hang out sometimes once you get home and get settled."

He accepted her offer as he watched her eat her salad. After taking a few sips of the ice cold water, she felt light thumps in her stomach. *I know this ain't what I think it is.* She sat perfectly still for a second until she felt it again. This time it was in two separate places. She squealed, causing Dallas to look at her crazy.

"What's wrong with you?"

She'd momentarily forgotten where she was when she placed both hands on her small round stomach. She wanted to feel her babies kick again.

"Yo Morgan, you alright?" Dallas walked over to her and sat next to her in the chair.

He wrapped his free arm around her shoulder. She had starting crying a few seconds after the kicks when she realized she couldn't share that moment with him. She nodded her head yes and packed up her lunch. She tried to leave, but he stopped her.

"Hold up Morgan. Tell me what's wrong." He removed her food from her hand, and pulled her into his arms. For a long time, she stood quietly until she built up the nerve to say she was pregnant. It took him a second to digest what she had just said, so he asked again for clarity.

"Say what now?"

"I'm pregnant, Dallas. I just felt my babies kick." Morgan scooted back so she could look into his face. She could tell by his expression that he was shocked, but it looked as if he was not only shocked but hurt as well. He backed away from her and sat on the corner of his bed. She sensed his withdrawal, so she asked him what was wrong. He looked at her; he needed answers.

"Why haven't you told me this before? I know I haven't said it, but you've had to know that I'm feeling you," Not knowing what to say, Morgan just stood there. "Why did you even let me fall for you if you knew you were pregnant with another man's child?"

Morgan couldn't believe him. The words coming out of his mouth hurt her to the core. Him not remembering her was getting exhausting, and she was tired of acting like she was fine with it. She was at her breaking point. She needed him as much as he needed her, and it was draining not having that support.

"Morgan, you've been pregnant all this time and didn't tell me? You didn't think I deserved to know? I know I can't remember us being together, but damn I ain't know you was with another nigga already." He was obviously angrier now and less hurt.

Morgan yelled back, she was just as angry as he was if not more.

● ● ●

"Dallas, why would I tell you I'm pregnant? What did that have to do with anything you have going on right now?"

"A LOT! Here I am falling for your ass and you ain't even got the decency to be honest with me." Listening to the things he were saying was so overwhelming that she had started crying again, and she hadn't noticed it until she felt the tears slide under her chin. The pain of his words was almost unbearable. When she gathered enough strength, she wiped her face and practically ran from his room. She couldn't believe he had accused her of cheating on him. She had been spending every free moment she had with him. From the day they met, it had been all about him, and he had the nerve to come at her like that? Oh no. He had her fucked all the way up. She was going to show him. She took out her phone and called Jade and Lay-Lay to tell them what happened.

Back in his room, Dallas stood looking out of the window; he couldn't believe he had actually let himself start falling for Morgan. That was a bad idea from the beginning, so this was his fault. He had been looking at their pictures and reading their text messages for the last couple of days, trying his hardest to gain something, but it just wasn't there. Now, to find out she's pregnant with the next nigga's seed was unendurable.

"Check my nigga out. Standing up and shit," Smoke laughed as he walked in Dallas' room. Dallas turned around to dap him up.

"When they letting you up out this muthafucka?" Smoke took a seat in the chair by the TV. Dallas told him his doctor said tomorrow as he went to sit on his bed.

"Well why the fuck you standing here looking all sad and shit? What's wrong with you?" Dallas let out a loud sigh and shook his head.

"You know my nurse Morgan, right?" Smoke nodded his head yeah, so Dallas continued

"Well she's pregnant. I mean it shouldn't matter to me because she isn't my woman, but that shit kind of fucked me up." Smoke looked at Dallas like he was crazy. He really *had* lost his mind.

"Dallas, it's about time for you to get this shit together, my dude. Morgan *is* your fucking woman. Y'all have been together for a while now. That's your damn baby that girl is having, nigga. What the fuck is wrong with you?"

Smoke had been his best friend for fifteen years, so he knew Smoke would give it to him straight. Dallas didn't know what to say.

"That's what everybody keeps telling me."

"Well believe it then nigga, damn! You see the fucking pictures. The girl is here every damn day, and I hope you didn't think it's because she's your nurse. How many of your other nurses be with you around the clock? That girl has been slaving like a dog at this fucking hospital so she can be close to you. You giving her your fucking ass to kiss ain't cool. At all." Smoke shook his head. "You better hope the babies she's carrying is all right. You be having that damn girl stressed the fuck out."

"Babies? How many she pregnant with?"

"Two. Y'all having twins, bruh. Where else you thought she's been getting all that ass from?"

That comment made Dallas laugh. He had been watching Morgan, and she was indeed getting thicker. He thought it was just all in his head, because he hadn't had sex in a while, but obviously it wasn't.

"You're a fool, but I have noticed it."

"You had started noticing it long before now. You were all paranoid and shit, trying to figure out if she was fucking somebody else when y'all weren't together and shit. I kept telling your ass she was probably pregnant." Smoke jogged a few memories in Dallas.

He remembered asking him and King that a few times. Dallas felt bad now. In the back of his mind, he had hoped she was pregnant by him, but he didn't want to take any chances. He thought about how mad Morgan was when she left; he had to make it up to her.

Chapter 8

Two weeks later and her eye still hadn't went completely down, but she needed to go grocery shopping. Tasheena tried to comb her bang over the swollen bruise above her left eye. Bam had been furious when he found out what happened, but she pleaded with him to just leave it alone. She wasn't very big on confrontation. She grabbed her purse and left the house. It was such a nice day outside that she'd almost hated that she'd be spending the rest of it in the house. On top of Bam being paranoid about Morgan, her face looked like she had gotten hit by a bus. Thankfully it was sunny outside, so her shades would hide most of it.

She hated the turn her life had taken. One day she was living on the beach in Virginia with her man spending money and having fun; the next, she was a widow before she could even get married. She wiped the tears that threatened to leave her eyes, and grabbed a cart out of the corner. Maybe shopping would free her mind. When Cameron was killed, it was like her world had shattered. They had been together since high school and were about to get married. She was five months pregnant with their son, Cameron junior, when some men broke into their house and shot him to death. She had barely made it out alive herself, but sadly baby Cameron hadn't. Cameron had just gotten put on with the Martinez Cartel, and was running things in Virginia.

• • •

The streets hated to see a young nigga make it, so they took it all away. They left her life in shambles in the process.

It seemed like drama surrounded her. All she wanted to do was live her life in peace, but that was proving to be a difficult task living with Bam. So lost in her thoughts, she didn't even see the lady walking in front of her buggy until it was too late. She slammed right into her, knocking her purse and cell phone on the floor. She apologized, letting her know she didn't see her there. She immediately bent down to help her retrieve the items that had fallen from her purse.

"It's okay, the supermarket is always crowded on pay day," she said, smiling at Tasheena.

The lady was a pretty light-skinned girl with dark brown hair and a nice skirt suit on.

"Oh wow you, work for the CIA? That must be so cool," Tasheena said, picking up her badge and handing it to her.

"Uh...yeah, it's alright, depending on what you like," she smiled, taking the rest of her things from Tasheena and stuffing them into her purse.

"I can understand that, sorry about running into you." Tasheena moved her cart and continued on with her shopping. The rest of the time she shopped, she daydreamed about her past life, and wished there was something she could do to get it back. Georgia was nice, but it wasn't home.

*****

"How's everything with Dallas?" one of D. Karter's wing men asked as they talked on the phone. D. Karter let him know that Dallas was making a good recovery, and he would be headed back home soon. His friend had been working with him for almost twenty years, and they had become more like family than friends. Anytime something went on with Dallas, D. Karter would ask him to tag along–from little league football games to when he met with his connects in Columbia to re-up. That was back when he was still in the drug game. D. Karter never allowed Dallas to make a move without his knowledge. He hadn't always been there up front, but he made sure to be a permanent part of the background. D. Karter looked around as he got out of the car, making sure he was aware of his surroundings; that was necessary at all times. Satisfied, he proceeded to the front door.

Before getting on the elevator, he decided to stop in the food court and grab him something to eat because he hadn't eaten all day. In the line, he stopped behind a lady looking to be in her mid-twenties. She had a tan skirt suit on. She was pretty, but not really his type. As he got closer to her in line, he noticed her turn around and glance at him over her shoulder. She spoke and he spoke back, letting her know she looked nice today. When she returned the compliment, she turned around to face him. D. Karter could tell she wanted small talk. He asked her what she was doing there on such a beautiful day.

"A friend of mine is here. What about you?" Marley twirled a piece of her hair as she talked.

"Here visiting my son."

"I hope he's alright. It was nice talking to you," she smiled again before walking away to give her order. The moment she got her food, she left.

Back in the restaurant, D. Karter was just about finished with his food when he noticed the pretty nurse he loved to flirt with. Today was his last day in the city, and he needed to get her number before he left. He wasn't trying to marry her or anything like that, but she looked like a fun girl to play around with. After throwing his food in the trash, he walked up behind her and snaked his hands around her waist. When he felt her hard round belly, he removed his hands and spun her around to face him.

"Get your hands off of me! I don't know who in the hell you think you are, or who I am for that matter, but don't touch me again." Morgan's face adorned a displeased look.

"I'm sorry sweetheart, I just thought maybe we could exchange numbers before I left tonight. But I see that might be a problem."

"You damn right it is. Don't be grabbing on me like that. I almost broke your fucking fingers off."

He didn't know what it was about this young girl, but she had him feeling challenged. He flashed that gorgeous smile and asked for her forgiveness. She told him it was cool before asking what it was that he wanted.

"First, I would like to know how far along you are. Next, do you think your man would mind if you brought his baby out to Cali for a little fun in the sun?"

Morgan couldn't help but smile; this man was such a flirt. She smiled harder as she prepared to burst his bubble.

"Being that my man is your son, he just may have a problem. Then again, who wouldn't want their kids to spend time with their granddaddy?" Standing back on one leg and crossing her arms, Morgan waited to see what kind of response he was about to give.

His head jerked back at her comment. He stood quiet for a second; nobody knew who he was. He made sure of that, so how in the hell did this girl know who his son was? He tried to deny her accusations by telling her she was mistaken.

"No sir, I don't think I am. You're Dallas Karter. Your son is Dallas Streeter in room 305. You visit him every night, and y'all look just alike." Morgan tapped her chin as if she was thinking about something, then continued. "You left him and his mother Marcy after she was attacked when he was eight years old. You were in charge of one of the largest drug rings on the west coast, and in order to keep your family safe, you had to leave. You're now the largest cocaine trafficker on the west coast, along with the southern regions. You're the man to see, Dallas Karter." D. Karter looked at her like she'd grown two heads, then he grabbed her by both arms and pushed her into the corner beside the vending machines.

"Listen little girl, who are you? You a fed or something?" Morgan smirked and played with a loose strand of her hair.

"No sir, I am not. I'm just a harmless nurse working my behind off to become a doctor one day."

One call was all she needed to make, and Jade had looked him up in her criminal database. Morgan didn't plan to use any of this information against him or anything like that; she actually kind of admired him.

"Who do you work for?" D. Karter squeezed her arms a little harder. Her face straightened and lost all traces of humor.

"I would advise you to get your hands off of me before I'm forced to break your wrist, Mr. Karter." He released her, but didn't move from his position, and asked her again who she worked for.

"Karter, I don't work for anybody. I just know some of the right people. I can promise you that your secret is safe with me. I just wanted to know more about you when I figured out who you were."

He stared at her for what seemed like forever before nodding his head and letting her out of the corner. For some reason, he believed her. He didn't know her from a can of paint, but his gut said that he could trust her.

"How do you know so much about me, and I don't even know your name?"

"My name is Morgan. I'm the love of your son's life as he is mine. I'm almost five months pregnant with our twins."

"Okay Miss Morgan, there has to be something you want from me in order to keep my secret. What is it?"

"I want us to be friends. If you're going to be sneaking around spying on my man, I at least want to know who you are. That's it. You have my word I will not try to bring any harm to you or your empire. I just want to make sure we're on the same page here." She stood on her tip toes so she could look him in the eye.

D. Karter chuckled at her silliness and leaned down to kiss her forehead. He rubbed her stomach once more and turned to leave, but before he could take two steps, he had to ask her how she'd found out about him. She winked and told him her best friend was a fed as she walked away. As he watched her leave, D. Karter had to admit his son had great taste in women. She was smart, successful, hard-core, and sexy as hell.

*****

Pressing the number two on his phone, Karter speed dialed the only other outsider he trusted with his secret. She answered almost immediately.

"Hello my sweetheart, how are you?"

"I'm pretty good. Can you talk right now?"

He could hear her scuffling around before coming back through the line. When she was calm again, she asked what was going on.

"This Morgan girl. Have you met her?"

"You're talking about Dallas' girlfriend right? Yes I've met her, she's perfect, isn't she?" Marcy's voice was full of love.

D. Karter expressed his amazement to Marcy. Marcy informed him that she and Dallas had been together for the last few months. When Marcy said Morgan was a sweetheart, D. Karter had to stop her. He ran off what had just happened between them at the hospital. Marcy was shocked, to say the least. No one knew about his secret.

"She told me her best friend is a fed, and all she wants is for us to be friends. I believe her."

"Oh yes. King's wife did just become an FBI agent. I forgot all about that. I told you sneaking into his room every night wasn't going unnoticed. He looks just like you."

"I know. I just didn't expect this. Did she tell you we're about to be grandparents?" He smiled at the thought. He couldn't wait until she had the babies. He actually might be ready to retire by then. They talked about the twins for a while before preparing to hang up. D. Karter had to get ready for his flight out.

"I'll catch you later Marcy, and thanks for keeping me informed. I love you, and tell Willie I said hello."

"No problem, Karter. I love you too, and I sure will. Goodbye."

Marcy hung up her phone. After all these years, she still loved D. Karter. He was her first love, and she'd do anything for him. When he left, he vowed to keep in touch, and that's exactly what he did. They tried staying together, but it just didn't work out with them never seeing each other. That's why she had moved on with Willie, and she was glad she had. She loved him, and he was a great father to Dallas, but sadly D. Karter would always have her heart. They had decided it was best to keep his secret away from Dallas so he could have a normal life with Willie, but Marcy was sure to keep him up to date with everything Dallas had going on.

*****

• • •

"I've been trying to keep tabs on D. Karter sir, but I haven't seen him anymore. He had been coming to the hospital every night, but I haven't seen him in two days." Marley reported to Arlington Taylor.

"What do you plan on doing, Agent Woods?" He was starting to grow tired of her and her helpless attitude. Anytime she couldn't figure something out, she would call him. Her next remark sounded defeated, but he didn't care.

"I'm going to find him sir."

"Okay, well keep me informed on your progress." He hung up.

He was packing for a business trip he had to make, and he didn't have time for Marley. Morgan had been calling every day with something new that she'd figured out, and pretty soon she was going to find out about Marley. When that time came, there would be close to nothing he could do to help her. After grabbing his badge and guns, he picked up his suitcase and walked out of his room. He had some other business he needed to tend to right now. He would worry about Marley when he got back–that is, if Morgan hadn't already gotten to her first.

After getting off the phone with her boss Marley called Bam to see if they could meet somewhere. She needed some help, and he was one of the only people she could trust right now. He hadn't answered the first few times she called, but he finally did around five calls later. He agreed to meet with her later that day. Marley took a breath and relaxed a little. This would all be over soon, and she could get back to her normal life. Dallas still didn't remember the thing he had with Morgan. Since he was getting released soon, she'd be out of their lives for a while, and Marley could make her move. Lying face down on her bed, she let her mind take her to thoughts of Dallas and the love they could possibly share.

*****

His doctor had just come sign his release papers, and Dallas was nothing short of excited. He had been in the hospital the past two months, and he was past ready to leave. Once he'd packed all of his things in his bag, Dallas buzzed the nurses' station and asked for Morgan. It had taken her such a long time to get there, he didn't think she would come. He knew she was still mad with him about yesterday, but he wanted to see her before he left. Just as he was unplugging his phone charger, she walked in the door. She was either just getting to work or getting ready to leave, because she was dressed in a pair of dark blue and pink palazzo pants with a pink shirt and some sandals. The shirt hugged her body close, displaying her small round belly and bulging belly button. Her hair was down and flipped in the front by her bangs.

She wore gold accessories and the same **MS** necklace she had on the other day.

"You needed me for something?" Morgan was giving him much attitude.

"Yeah, I was just letting you know I was about to leave. I wanted to see if the offer about us hanging out when I got home still stands."

Dallas was standing there in his khaki polo shorts and white V-neck shirt–how could she deny him? He was so sexy she couldn't stand it. She smiled and rolled her eyes. He smiled as he walked to her and grabbed her hand. When he sat on the bed, he pulled her onto his lap and began rubbing her stomach.

"I'm sorry about the other day, M. Your pregnancy caught me off guard."

"Imagine how I felt finding out I was pregnant on the same day my boyfriend came to the hospital almost dead. With not one, but two babies. I was pretty caught off guard myself, Mr. Streeter." Cynicism dripped off of her every word. He asked her to forgive him. The more he thought about how hard it must have been on her, the worse he felt. He could sense she still had an attitude, so he leaned up and kissed her neck. He slid his hands from her stomach and rubbed up between her thighs.

"Dallas please don't. I can't take it." She hurriedly jumped off of his lap. He held her by her waist in front of him. He leaned forward and kissed her stomach through her shirt. After kissing all around it a few times, he replaced his mouth with his hands.

"Come on. Move for daddy."

Morgan didn't know what is was about Dallas' voice, but the moment after he said it, her stomach began to jump in different places. Dallas beamed with excitement.

"Ah shit! Look M, they're moving!"

Everywhere he saw a movement he would lean forward and kiss it. Observing how excited he was about their babies made Morgan cry. She'd been wanting this from the time she found out about her pregnancy, and it was finally coming true.

"My babies know their daddy." Dallas stood up and wrapped his arms around Morgan's shoulders. "You're such a fucking crybaby, Morgan." He kissed the top of her head as he pulled her into a much needed hug. "So I guess since I'm your baby daddy I'm entitled to some pregnant pussy, right?" he released her from his arms.

"Your mouth is so filthy Dallas."

"I'm saying though Morgan, a nigga ain't had sex in a good two months from what I can remember. I know you ain't trying to hold out."

"Can we get some food first, then talk about that?"

• • •

She was so happy he was back to his old self, minus the fact he still had no recollection of them ever being a couple. She guessed that would come eventually.

"Yeah, I guess we can discuss this over some lunch."

"Good. Can you carry your bag or you need me to get it?" Dallas frowned at her outstretched arm and pushed it back down.

"Morgan, what do I look like letting your pregnant ass carry this bag?" Morgan turned around with her hand on her small belly.

"Well excuse me, I just wanted to make sure you didn't put too much stress on your body that's all."

Dallas rubbed his hand across her butt. "How about you worry about me putting too much stress on your body?"

"Whew boy. Come on, let's get out of this hospital room before I give you what you're asking for."

They held hands and left his room.

Once downstairs in Morgan's jeep, they decided to go to a small restaurant in Atlantic Station to have lunch. It took them a little while to get there. Once parked, they got out and headed up the stairs to where all of the restaurants were.

Watching Morgan walk with a slight wobble was the cutest thing Dallas had ever seen. She looked so pretty pregnant, even though he still couldn't remember what they shared before he could definitely feel a new love blooming. He grabbed her hand and brought it to his waiting lips.

"You look so fucking gorgeous Morgan."

"So do you Dallas."

After deciding to sit outside on the patio, they placed their orders and waited for their food. Dallas had been cooped up inside hospital rooms for the last few months, so he welcomed the fresh air. Atlantic Station was always so lively when the weather was nice. Music was playing, stores were booming, and plenty of people occupied the streets. Morgan and Dallas were busy talking and laughing when somebody rode past blasting Snootie Wild's "She's a Keeper." It was as if time had stopped. So much was going on around them, but all he saw was her. Morgan noticed the zoned out look on his face, and immediately became concerned. He listened closely, waiting for a familiar part to come up.

"What's wrong Dally?"

"*I'm tryna build something, win with you, Hope this shit here never ever end with ya.*" He rapped to her.

His eyes were fixed on her as he listened intently to the rest of the song. Although he didn't sing anymore of the song, that was all he needed to hear. Everything hit him at once. He lunged across the table, nearly knocking it over. Dallas grabbed her in a hug and kissed her. He kissed her face over and over while holding her tight. She wrapped her arms around his waist and pulled him to her.

"Dally, what's wrong baby? What are you doing?"

Instead of letting her go, he squeezed tighter. When she turned her head slightly, she felt moisture on the side of her face. He was crying. Morgan held him tighter as she listened to his muffled sniffles. She begged for him to tell her what was wrong, but he wouldn't say anything. She didn't understand. One minute they were laughing and talking, and now he was crying in front of everybody–not to mention he was about to squeeze the life out of her. Although not many people were looking at them, it still felt like it. Once Dallas finally loosened his hold, Morgan pulled back and he cradled her face between his hands. He looked at her beautiful face. He took in every inch of her beauty. From her small round eyes, to the newly established wideness of her nose. Morgan had always been gorgeous to him, but his babies were magnifying it. She'd never looked better to him than she did right then.

"I remember Morgan. I remember us now."

Morgan felt like her heart was about to pop out of her chest. She had been waiting on this for two months.

"That song. When I heard it, my mind got foggy. Then you called me Dally, and it all made sense. I love you, baby girl. I remember now, I really remember." He pulled her into his hard chest again. Morgan held him as close as her stomach would allow. She laid her head on his chest and listened to his heartbeat while he ran his hands through her hair. After pulling away, they returned to their seats but continued holding hands. Dallas looked across the table at her and smiled the biggest smile he could muster.

"I love you."

"I love you too. I knew you would come back to me." She smiled and blew him a kiss. Finally! Things had gotten back to normal. Prayerfully, it would only get better.

Chapter 9

Bam stopped his car and got out. He walked to meet Marley in front of the Verizon store. She has asked to see him so they could talk. They decided to meet in Atlantic Station. It was the closest place between the two of them. He looked back at his car to make sure Tasheena was okay, and continued up the sidewalk. He had been making her stay in the house for the past couple of weeks to make sure she was safe. When she asked to ride with him today, he obliged. Spotting Marley on a bench next to the food bistros, he went and took a seat next to her.

"What's up, what you needed to talk to me about?" Her body jumped at the sound of his voice.

"Damn Brice! You scared me."

Bam didn't bother to offer any apologies. He remained quiet until she started talking again.

"Well as you know, this shit with Dallas has gotten completely out of control. I need your help. I know I didn't follow through on my end of the deal this last time, but I promise I got you this time. I'll even pay you before you do anything."

"You're talking in circles, Marley. What is it that you need?" Bam looked off into the distance, observing the passing patrons.

"There's this man named D. Karter. I need you to keep your ear to the streets and see if you can find out his whereabouts."

"All right I got you." He stood to leave.

He didn't even give her a chance to say anything else as he headed back to his car. He had no intentions of helping her do anything else. There was no need to hear anything else she had to say. He was done with her. He thought maybe she had his money or something, but all she wanted was to use him again. Shaking his head, he hopped back in his car and pulled off.

"You're working with the feds now?" Tasheena hadn't even waited for him to sit down before talking. With his face scrunched in confusion, he turned to his sister. He asked her why she would ask him that; she should have known better.

"That girl is the police. The one you were talking to."

"No she isn't."

"Yes she is. I bumped into her one day at the grocery store and knocked her purse over. Her badge fell out. She works for the CIA. When we first pulled up, I couldn't remember where I knew her from until she turned around and watched you walk to the car."

Bam couldn't believe his ears. Marley had been gone for a while, and Tasheena wouldn't lie about anything that serious. He cursed as he cranked his car up. Shit was getting all kinds of crazy now. Bam didn't know what to do or which way to turn next.

*****

"You sure that was him?" Morgan and Dallas were walking back to her car.

"Yeah. That's the same Impala they put me in that night at the hotel. I know it is because I looked at that big ass USC sticker on the back of his window." She and Dallas were busy having their lunch when he spotted Marley across the street talking to Jade's ex-boyfriend, Bam. They watched them sit and talk for a good five minutes before he walked off and got into a black Impala. Morgan and Dallas conversed, trying to figure out why those two of all people would be talking. Her mind was going a mile a minute; her mental wheels had started turning the moment she saw them talking. Morgan pulled out her cell phone and called Jade and Lay-Lay on 3-way. After running down the story real quick for her girls, Morgan tried to get their thoughts on the situation. The shock in their voices was evident. The three talked about how ironic this incident was when Jade told Morgan Zion and KB had found Antoine for her. Morgan ranted about how she was going to get him the entire drive to her house. Dallas interrupted her conversation.

"Morgan, you're pregnant. Let me handle this shit."

Morgan looked from him to the road. "No. You are more than welcome to come with me, but you better believe I'm about to get to the bottom of this."

"Okay, but under one condition. Whatever we do, we do it together. You don't do shit without me."

Morgan gave him her word before going back to her phone call. The three friends made plans to meet up and go see Antoine together. Jade had to wait until King got home from work, but Lay-Lay was ready right then. Morgan told Lay she'd pick her up on the way, and they ended their call. Once inside her apartment, Dallas stood there for a minute. He wanted to take it all in. Morgan knew he needed a minute, but he'd have to get that later. Her sex drive was through the roof. She began sliding out of her pants when she noticed his attention was on her. Dallas' face was lust-filled as his manhood began to rise.

"I'm about to go take a shower, you coming?

"Hell yeah I'm coming!" He pulled his shorts off the best he could.

Morgan could see he was still in a little pain, so she moved towards him. She helped him pull his shirt and shoes off. As they walked down the hallway to her bathroom, Morgan pulled the remainder of her garments off and turned the shower on. While she was standing in the mirror to wrap her hair, Dallas walked up behind her and kissed down the back of her neck. His lips

• • •

made her whole body shiver. She gripped the sides of her sink and leaned forward so she could give him access to her neck. Dallas rubbed his hands across her nipples and began sucking on her neck. He had her moaning like crazy. It had been months since she had sex, and being pregnant made it worse. She was always so wet and horny.

"I missed you Dally," she moaned as he picked her up and sat her on the counter top.

Morgan wrapped her arms around his neck and sucked on his lips. Dallas was all for foreplay, but he wanted Morgan right then—that would have to wait until later. He grabbed her butt and scooted her to the edge of the sink. He positioned himself at her opening and rubbed it around her moist heat; he looked into her eyes while he did that. Morgan thought her body would combust into a hot flame if he didn't hurry up.

"Put it in Dallas." He was driving her crazy with lust. She didn't know how much more she was going to be able to take.

Dallas leaned his forehead against Morgan's as he put just the tip in. She was so hot and wet. He lifted both of her legs until they rested in the crooks of his arms. He steadied himself before pushing deep inside of her.

"Owww Dally!" her scream echoed off of the walls. She had forgotten how big he was. His husky voice filled her ear.

"I'm sorry baby."

Stroking her slow and steady, Dallas made sure Morgan felt every inch of him. He moaned in her ear as he got lost in her pussy. It was clinching around him with so much need and hunger. Her insides were pulling him deeper with each stroke.

"You missed me Morgan?" He watched her throw her head back against the mirror.

Morgan moaned quietly. It was so low it was almost childlike. Her eyes were closed, and her face was twisted in pleasure. He smiled confidently as he watched her unravel before him. Her body was made just for him. Her pussy welcomed him; between her thighs was his new home. There would never be another man that could make her feel like he did. He pushed harder, causing her eyes to pop open. Dallas could tell he was in deep by the way she squeezed her muscles tighter around him. She moaned his name as her eyes rolled back. Speeding up a little, he could feel Morgan's body starting to relax, which caused her to get wetter.

"Cum for me Morgan. I want you to cum all over my dick."

She was so wet that his stomach and thighs were covered in her juices. Dallas was hitting it so good that Morgan started mumbling stuff he couldn't even understand. Feeling she was near an orgasm, he picked up his speed a little, making sure to hit her spot. He kept his pace steady as he continued hitting her spot. She started coming and screaming all at once.

"That's right baby girl. Don't hold back." Dallas looked down at the creamy white stuff covering his dick.

She kissed all over his neck and chest as her orgasm subsided. She held onto him tightly as he came a few seconds later. He was so weak from the knee buckling orgasm he'd just had that he collapsed on top of her. Morgan immediately began pushing him off of her.   "Dallas, baby you have to get up. You can't lay on me like this. You're squishing my stomach."

He was so tired that instead of walking to the shower, he slid down to the floor and sat there for a minute.

Morgan slid off of the sink and hopped in the shower. Her pussy was sore and her legs were weak, but she had stuff to do. Dallas always had her hurting after sex. She didn't complain though, because it was a good hurt–the kind that made you smile every time you thought about why you were in pain in the first place. She smiled as she rinsed her body and cut off the shower. On her way out of the bathroom, she stepped over Dallas. In her room, she got dressed in all black and combed her hair back down.

By now, Dallas had gotten up and was getting out of the shower. Once in her room, she watched him grab some clothes from the closet as well, and then head to the spare bedroom to get the stuff they would need for the night. Fully dressed, Morgan walked into the spare bedroom to find Dallas loading guns. She leaned down as best as she could beside him, without squishing her stomach, and grabbed her favorite knife. She strapped it to her holster. Dallas shook his head.

"I don't know why you like that fucking thing."

"Because I'm good with it. By the time they realize I have it, they'll be almost dead—a stab wound straight to the heart."

She was making jokes, but she really was good with her knife. Her dad had taught her so much stuff she could do with it. She almost preferred it over her guns; knives were just a lot messier. Dressed and ready, the couple left the house to pick up Lay-Lay. Having talked to Jade and King already, Morgan told Dallas they would meet them there. The two held hands as Morgan continuously tried to convince Dallas this wasn't too much strain on her or the babies. Normally all this nagging would get on her nerves, but not now. She was too happy to have him back, and even happier to have him share in her joy. He was being overprotective, but he meant well. Morgan could tell he was happy to be a father. They were so caught up in their own conversation that Lay thought maybe they'd forgotten she was in the car. She thought it was sweet, but decided to interrupt them anyway.

"Dallas I'm so glad you finally got your shit together. Morgan's crying ass was getting on my last nerve." Dallas laughed as he gave Morgan's hand a light squeeze.

"She was that bad, Lay-Lay?"

"HELL YES! I can't count how many times I was about to slap her ass."

Morgan laughed along with Lay-Lay and Dallas. She knew she had it bad, so she didn't even try to deny it. Dallas' smiling face made her the happiest she had been in months.

"I can't help how deep in love I am with Dallas." She watched as he started blushing.

She knew he would. Anytime she would say something like that, he would blush. She thought it was the cutest thing ever. It was amazing how a man as hardcore as Dallas could be so sweet at the same time. Morgan soon noticed they had gotten to the old barn. This was where Zion and KB had left Antoine. Dallas made sure both women were ready before exiting the truck.

Upon entering the barn, they could tell Zion and KB had already beat up on Antoine. One of his eyes was swollen, and his mouth was bleeding. His wrists were tied together with a rope that was linked through a chain hanging from the ceiling. The rope was lowered enough for his feet to touch the ground, so he was standing. Morgan took the lead and walked over to him first. She then grabbed his face to make him look at her. She told him to wake up as she lifted his head up. He made eye contact with Morgan and held it. He nodded his head yes when Morgan asked did he know why he was there.

"I got your name from a friend of mine, but for some reason she couldn't tell me who you were working with. You think you could help me out with that?"

"It was my nigga Brice."

"Brice as in Bam?" Lay-Lay asked, and he nodded.

Dallas stood back and allowed Morgan to handle this her way. He'd told her he would only step in if she needed him to. She took advantage of the fact that he liked watching her in action.

"So why, out of all people, did y'all want to fuck with my man?"

"It wasn't a personal debt with us. Some bitch asked him to do it. She said she would pay us, but she never did." Morgan wanted to know why, but he didn't know.

"I don't even know what she looks like. Bam asked did I want to make some money. He said all I had to do was help him beat somebody up, and then we would get the loot."

Morgan walked around until she was standing directly in front of him and asked where she could find

Bam. Antoine looked down at his pants as he ran off Bam's address. He offered his phone to them as well so they could get his number. After reaching into his pockets, Lay-Lay produced his cell phone and stuck it in her purse; they'd use that later.

"Because you were such a big help, I'm not going to kill you. However, I am going to have my little brothers beat your ass some more. Something similar to what you and Bam did to my baby." She texted Zion for him and KB to go back to the barn as she, Lay-Lay, and Dallas turned to leave. Lay-Lay and Dallas followed behind her as she pushed the big door open. Neither of them said anything until they were back in the car. Morgan texted Jade letting her know they were done already and they didn't need to come. Lay-Lay took out Antoine's phone and texted Bam asking was he home so they could stop by.

When he responded back yeah, they headed in that direction. Lay-Lay was surprised that the directions were to the same little house they'd visited a few weeks ago. The drive wasn't a long one, but it gave them all a few minutes to relax. Dallas turned into the driveway and killed the engine, and they all got out. Morgan knocked on the door and waited for an answer. When no one came, she knocked again, this time a little harder. Finally the door opened, and just like last time, Morgan forced her way into the house. Tasheena stood there with nothing but her sweats and tank top on. You could hear the nervousness in her voice when she asked them what they needed. This time Dallas spoke.

"Where's your brother at?" His deep voice carried through the small living room.

Just as he finished his question, Bam came hopping down the stairs. He was asking his sister who was at the door when he stopped mid-sentence. He almost fell when he saw Dallas, Morgan, and Lay-Lay standing in his living room. Dallas pulled his gun out and pointed it at Bam.

"Don't get scared now, pussy."

Morgan took a seat on the couch before motioning for Bam to follow. He was hesitant about turning his back on Dallas at first, but eventually obliged.

"Who paid you to kidnap Dallas?" Her tone was calm. She had been feeling a little weak ever since they left the barn, and she didn't want to overexert herself. The further along she got in her pregnancy, the more her body changed. It was new to her, but she knew when to take it easy.

"Why?" Bam was trying to act tough.

Dallas walked closer to him and pressed the gun to the side of his head. He chuckled a little at Bam's audacity. "Right now ain't the time to act hard."

Tasheena screamed for him to tell them the truth. It was obvious she was scared for her brother's life. Lay-Lay laughed at how dramatic she was being.

* * *

"A girl named Marley." Bam looked over at his sister before answering.

"Did she say why she wanted this done?" Dallas looked from Bam to Morgan, instantly noticing Morgan was sweating profusely. "Aye shawty, get my girl some water and something to eat on. Lay-Lay, go with her."

Tasheena led the way, with Lay-Lay following close behind her. Dallas wanted to make sure she didn't do anything to Morgan's food or water. He wanted to ask questions, but he needed to make sure his girl and his babies were good first.

"You all right, baby?"

"Yeah baby I'm good, just a little tired, that's all. Handle this so we can go." She removed her gun from her waistband and laid it on the table so she could lie back comfortably. Dallas went back to questioning Bam, this time with a little more urgency.

"Look nigga did she say why?"

"At first she said it was to rob you. Then she said she didn't want any of the money, so I knew that had to be a lie. Eventually, she told me it was to make you love her or some shit like that. The other day when I went to meet her, my sister told me she works for CIA."

Bam's comment gathered a confused look from both Dallas and Morgan. Morgan sat up abruptly. She was glad they'd returned with her food; the babies and this news was about to make her pass out.

"You mean like the police CIA?" Morgan took a bite of the sandwich and thanked Tasheena.

"Yeah. My sister said she saw her at the store and her badge fell out of her purse."

This confused Dallas, because she'd told him she was a schoolteacher. Bam went on to explain that he'd known Marley for a while, and she could be a little crazy at times. He told them that although she'd never told him she was the police, he believed his sister. Dallas ran his hands across his head, trying to make sense of everything. He had been out of the dope game for some time now, so she couldn't be on him about that. He racked his brain, but came up with nothing.

"Tasheena come on, you're going with us until I can get this shit straightened out. Bam, don't do any fly shit. I won't hesitate to kill her ass." Morgan got off of the sofa and grabbed her gun.

Tasheena slid on her flip flops and followed Morgan out of the house. Morgan could tell she was scared, but she'd be okay. She was grown; she needed to be able to handle situations like this. Dallas followed behind Morgan, but Lay-Lay stopped for a minute.

"Bam, this is some grimey shit you're into my boy. You need to get your shit together and go back to playing ball. This street life ain't even for you. You're not built for this shit, so stop pretending before you fuck around and get into some shit you can't get out of." She looked at him long and hard before walking away. Bam held his head in his hands. He knew Lay-Lay was telling the truth. Ever since he had left school, he had been getting into the wrong stuff.

Chapter 10

Arlington Taylor walked through the airport and looked around for his longtime partner and friend. His buddy had called him earlier that week asking him to take a trip to Columbia with him to handle some business. Never the one to leave a friend hanging, Arlington agreed. He had brushed past a ton of strangers and suitcases before he finally spotted his friend in the back. The two exchanged greetings before walking to his buddy's car. Upon settling into the front seat, Arlington felt his phone vibrate. He checked the caller ID and noticed it was Marley. She said she really needed to speak with him. Arlington checked his watch and realized he had time to spare, so he arranged for her to meet with him. She was shocked to hear he was in Atlanta, but was still happy. She thought maybe he could help her with her case in person.

Arlington held the bridge of his nose with his thumb and forefinger. "That's one agent that's not making it through training. After this case she's done."

"She's that bad?"

"Worse!" Arlington took this time to explain just how sloppy she was.

While Arlington was busy dealing with his messy agent, Morgan was across town dealing with her as well. How ironic was it that Marley Woods was a problem for them both. Morgan wanted so badly to get a good hold

• • •

on her, but that didn't look like it was about to happen. She, Dallas, Lay-Lay, and Tasheena were riding to her house in hopes of her being there. Just as they were pulling up to Marley's house, they noticed her getting into her car.

"You want to follow her?" Morgan looked over at Dallas.

"Yeah, let's see where she's going." Dallas merged into traffic behind her.

They followed her for a few blocks until they reached downtown. They waited five minutes after she walked away to get out of the car and trail her. They entered a hotel behind her after making sure all of their weapons were concealed. She stood at the front desk for a few minutes before leaving and walking towards the ball room. Once they got there, they peaked inside the window to be sure she was alone before going in. The massive room was completely empty besides the tables and chairs in the back.

"Lay-Lay, Dallas and I will go in first. You watch the door for about ten minutes to make sure nobody else is following us, then you and Tasheena come in."

Lay-Lay agreed as she and Tasheena headed back towards the bathroom. It was at the front of the building near the entrance, while the ballroom was down the hall in the back. It was a good thing the room was relatively secluded, that way they could have some privacy. Once they were sure Lay-Lay and Tasheena were gone, Dallas opened the door for Morgan and stood to the side so she could walk in first. When Marley heard the door open, she turned around with wide eyes. She was extremely surprised to see Morgan and Dallas. Morgan was already headed towards her.

"Don't look scared now, lil bitch."

"What are y'all doing here?" Not only was she scared of Morgan killing her, but if she didn't and her boss showed up, her career was over.

"We'll be asking the questions today. You've done your share of causing problems. I would advise you to hush for right now." Morgan stopped directly in front of her.

Marley looked past Morgan at Dallas. "Dallas, what's going on?"

Morgan balled her fist up and hit Marley in her nose. "Don't disrespect me again, talking to my man like you don't see me standing here. That's your problem now–there is no more you and him. Anything you have to say to him, it goes through me first. Remember that." Morgan watched her wipe the blood from her lip. "Now back to the reason we're here. Why in the hell did you hire somebody to kidnap and beat Dallas? What did you call yourself trying to do?"

Marley's eyes started to water. She let out a whole dramatic scene about how she just wanted him to love her again; this angered Morgan and Dallas beyond words. He could have died over her psychotic feelings. He was so angry that he was halfway to her when Morgan held up her hand to stop him. Morgan whipped her gun out and start beating Marley across the face with it. Blood spewed from her nose instantly. Morgan hadn't intended on doing anything strenuous, but once she heard Marley's excuse, all she saw was red–she was so angry. Her body had gotten hot, and her hands had begun shaking. Her heart was beating so fast in her chest; it was like she could hear it in her ears. Marley cowered over, trying to cover her face with her arms to no avail. Morgan was hitting her anywhere the gun landed. Marley's screams only magnified the raging infuriation inside of her.

"Yo bae, chill! You can't be doing this shit." Dallas pulled her away just as the door to the ballroom opened up.

Morgan was so furious she kept her eyes glued to Marley. She didn't even bother to turn around. When Marley looked up, her eyes got big. She spat a mouth full of blood on the floor so she could speak.

"I can explain sir."

"There's no need for explanations."

Morgan froze in place when she heard her father's voice. *It can't be.*

"Morgan, turn around." She heard him say.

Alongside Morgan's shocked face, there was Dallas' and Marley's too. Arlington had caught all three of them off guard for three totally different reasons. Morgan smiled when she finally turned and locked eyes with her father. She squealed in excitement as she ran to him. He scooped her up into a long hug.

"Hey Daddy!"

Daddy? What the fuck? Dallas thought to himself.

She had just asked him what he was doing there, when he reached down and rubbed her small belly. He asked her the same question in return. He didn't approve of her being in these types of situations while she was carrying his grandchildren. They were so caught up in one another they'd briefly forgotten they weren't alone–that was until both of their faces turned up in disdain at the sound of Marley's voice.

"Sir, Morgan is your daughter?"

"Yes she is, Agent Woods."

Morgan couldn't believe she'd even asked something that dumb. She'd been there while they were talking, so it was obvious.

"Hold on Daddy, so you mean to tell me this sloppy piece of woman right here really is the CIA?" Morgan was very displeased.

"Well, yes and no, baby girl. She was a member until she failed her training so no, not anymore." He clarified for both her and Marley.

* * *

Marley was on the verge of tears as she asked what she'd done wrong. Arlington let her know she was sloppy and too emotional for this type of job. Morgan smiled at the look on Marley's face as she wrapped her free arm around her father. Morgan decided to rub it in a little, further letting him know she could have fired Marley for him a long time ago. The more she talked, the sadder Marley appeared to be. She basked in Marley's disappointment until a terrible thought crossed her mind. She asked because she needed clarity.

"So you knew all along what was going to happen to Dallas?"

He carefully explained that he would have never given an order for her to do something that reckless. That too aided in Marley's dismissal from the force. Morgan breathed a sigh of relief. It would have taken some time for her to get over that one.

Morgan watched her father look from Marley to Dallas. Morgan could see the anger in Dallas' face. Arlington asked Dallas what the problem was, only to be ignored. Arlington smirked slightly at Dallas' childish behavior. Morgan observed the whole situation. She knew her father as much as she knew Dallas. They were both bullheaded. Morgan waited for Dallas to answer her father, but it never came. Instead, he began speaking to her.

"Morgan, did you know your father is a drug trafficker?"

Morgan stepped away from her dad so she could see his face. She was in total disbelief. "You traffic drugs, Daddy?"

"No my sweet girl, I do not. My partner does."

"He's lying Morgan. I've seen him numerous of times when I went to speak with my connects. He was in Columbia every time." Dallas spoke through clenched teeth. Clearly the vein in his neck was on a rampage; it was thumping all over the place.

Morgan asked her father for an explanation. He told her to give him a second and he'd explain everything. Arlington took out his phone and dialed his partner's number. He asked him to come in before hanging up. After a few moments, the door opened again, and in walked his partner. *This can't be real,* Morgan thought as she lost her balance and fell into Dallas. After catching her, he picked her up and sat her in the chair at the table next to him. Her father and his partner both ran to her aid, but were quickly cut off by Dallas.

"GET THE FUCK BACK!" He yelled at them both, letting them know he had her.

He was past angry. If they weren't in a public hotel, there would have already been two dead bodies. Both men took a few steps back to allow Morgan to get herself together. Dallas snatched a menu from the table and stood up to fan her. It took her a moment to refocus her eyes. Her vison was blurred, and she was lightheaded. She finally got it together and stood up slowly, with Dallas holding onto her waist. He pulled her back against his chest so she could use him to maintain her balance. She felt secure in his strong arms.

"I'm all confused. Daddy, why are you affiliated with D. Karter?" She rubbed the top of Dallas hands.

They were resting on her stomach and had tightened around her briefly before loosening again. She could tell by the way he was shaking that he recognized his father and he was livid. Her father told her he and Karter went way back, and had been partners for the last twenty years.

"So basically, you're saying you are a drug dealer? I know his background, and it's not good." She continued to rub Dallas' hands. She could feel him getting madder by the second.

"Listen Morgan, because I'm only going to say this once. Karter and I are partners on the force. He is an undercover agent. Everything you think you know about him has been placed there. He's too far undercover, and has been for years. He runs the majority of the drug rings here in the United States."

Morgan couldn't believe what she was hearing. Apparently she wasn't the only one. Dallas' deep voiced boomed behind her.

"So this is why you couldn't stay and be a father?"

D. Karter shook his head and sighed. "Dallas, it's way more complicated than you think. Contrary to what you may believe, I've been there your whole life. I haven't missed a beat, son."

Dallas remained silent. Morgan waited for his response, but it never came. The only thing he did was rub her hard, round stomach. Morgan knew he would never leave her and their children. His silence was familiar to her. Morgan had grown to learn that his method of protection from hurt was to shut down. His silence proved that. There would be no more talking to D. Karter for him. She was just going to have to explain it to him later, and hope they could make amends. She could see now that there were absolutely no chances of that happening in that ballroom. Morgan took a seat, this was too much to take in at once.

"Dallas, I'm really sorry you had to find out like this." D. Karter stared into Dallas' stoic face. Morgan held up her hand to silence D. Karter.

"Just be quiet. I got him."

She stood back up with Dallas' help and wrapped her arms around his waist; there that vein was again, thumping in the side of his neck like crazy.

"Look at me, Dally." It took him a moment, but when he looked down into her face, he relaxed a little.

● ● ●

"It's alright baby. We got this, okay? Calm down and just take it all in." She pulled his face down so she could kiss his lips. His face remained hard, but she could feel his body loosening up.

"So what was my part in all of this, sir?" Marley reminded everybody of her presence.

She had been standing off to the side, watching everything unfold. She too had known Dallas' issues with his father. He talked about it a lot when they were together in high school.

"Agent Woods, D. Karter wanted to personally meet his son. You were supposed to arrange something to bring them together. Instead of thinking of something sensible, you almost killed this man." Arlington shook his head in disapproval. "Morgan, we have to go now because there's a flight we have to catch, but we'll be flying back in tomorrow evening. I would love to have lunch with my baby," Arlington smiled at her. Smiling back at him, Morgan walked over to give him a hug. As he hugged her, he whispered in her ear.

"Everything that was said today is classified information. No one else can know about it." He kissed the side of her head and released her. He turned to leave, but before he left, he turned back to face her. "Morgan, remember when I said it was classified?"

She looked at him, ready and waiting for his next words. "Yes sir, Daddy."

"Can you do daddy a favor and make sure it stays that way?" He looked into her eyes; she understood right away. Morgan pulled out her knife, and in one swift move, she threw it into the center of Marley's chest. Blood shot out just before Marley's now lifeless body fell to the floor. Arlington winked at his daughter and headed for the doors. Before he and D. Karter could get to them, the doors to the ballroom opened and in ran Tasheena with a gun. Dallas and Morgan both pulled their guns and pointed them at her.

"You bastard, I'm going to kill you!" She lunged forward with her finger on the trigger.

Morgan ran towards her. "Tasheena NOOOOOOOO!"

Dallas was right behind her, trying to block her from Tasheena's line of fire.

POP! POP! It was too late. Shots were fired and bodies had fallen.

Chapter 11

Morgan sat in one of the chairs in the ballroom, bouncing her leg. She ran her hand through her hair for the hundredth time since the shooting. No matter how hard she tried, she just couldn't wrap her mind around what had just happened. Dallas didn't know if it was the twins, or if it really was too much going on. Either way, she needed a bed–and quick. It looked like she would pass out at any given moment. Dallas stood next to her rubbing her forehead with a cold washcloth. Lay-Lay had brought it to them the second time Morgan passed out. The EMT's that had just left, making sure everything was okay with her and the babies before departing. Dallas watched her as she rocked back and forth in the chair. If he didn't get a handle on this situation quick, Morgan was going to break down. She had been dealing with a lot over the past few months, and today's activities hadn't helped. All the stress she was enduring couldn't be good for his twins, so he would have to get out of his feelings for a second. He took a knee next to Morgan and placed his hand on her stomach.

"Stop stressing my babies out before I kick your ass." She stopped bouncing her leg and snickered a little. "I'll handle all of this, okay? Just be cool and relax. Daddy will take y'all home in a minute." Dallas smiled when he saw her smile.

He kissed her stomach twice before kissing her lips and standing up. When he turned around, he walked to the front of the ballroom and where Lay-Lay was sitting with Tasheena, and sent Lay-Lay to sit with Morgan. He needed answers before he made any moves. Tasheena's face was covered in tears and snot as she cried. Her hair was all over the place, and she looked zoned out. Dallas sat next to her and offered her a bottle of water. It took her a moment to realize he had taken Lay-Lay's spot on the floor next to her. She took the water and the tissue he handed her, and tried to clean herself up. She wiped her face roughly until it was dry. Although there were no more tears falling, her eyes were still watery. You could tell she was in pain, and Dallas needed to know why. He sat quietly, waiting for her to say something. After a good ten minutes, another tear fell and she started talking.

"Before I moved here, I was pregnant and engaged to my child's father. We were high school sweethearts, and we were so in love. Cameron had just gotten put on with a major cartel, and people started hating. He was making power moves, and the streets couldn't take it. One night we were sleeping, and our house was invaded. There were four men, and they shot up the place. By the time they reached our room, Cameron had gotten his guns and put me into the closet. Something in me told me he was about to die. Even when he promised me he was going to be fine, I knew it was a lie. I sat in our bulletproof closet, watching him on the small security screen as he tried to take out all of them by himself. He had almost made it out when another one walked in and shot him in the head. I watched his body jerk from the bullets as he was gunned down. The man that killed him wasn't wearing a mask. I saw his face.   "It has been embedded in my memory since then. That night I miscarried, alone, in our safe room. The next day when I woke up, I was in a hospital bed. Our neighbors had called the police, and they found me in the closet," Tasheena pushed her hair from her face. "I had passed out from blood loss. I was miserable. I cried every day. They had to place me into the psychiatric ward for three months until my father came and got me. I've been here trying to piece my life back together ever since. My fiancé's killer was the man that I shot earlier. I hope he dies." Tasheena turned to look at Dallas. His face was sympathetic. He pitied her situation, because it was a tough one. It was even worse for a woman her age.

"I don't think he's going to die. You hit him once in the shoulder and once in the side, but both were flesh wounds. My girl cleaned him up pretty good, he'll be fine. Tasheena, he's my father."

Her eyes were wide with fear, then replaced with sympathy of her own.

"I had no idea he was your father. I just wanted to kill him. All the unnecessary drama we've put you through has me rethinking my feelings now. By no means do I regret my attempted retribution, but I don't want to add anymore strife to your life. I'm sorry, Dallas."

He promised her it was fine before he got up to check on Morgan again. Dallas thought back on the scene that had just happened. When Tasheena ran in shooting, his intent was to stop her. He hesitated when he saw who she was gunning for. For a moment, he too wanted her to kill D. Karter, but he hadn't and neither had Tasheena. She was such a lousy shot she only grazed his flesh both times.

The moment it happened, Morgan was on him checking his wounds. When she realized it wasn't life threatening, she sent Lay-Lay to get a first aid kit and patched him up. He and Arlington had left for their flight shortly afterwards. In the end, Arlington being there turned out for the best. Once Tasheena had come in shooting, the police had been called. Of course, Arlington was able to get them out with no trouble through his CIA affiliation. God was really providing today, because the police came right after Mack had come and picked Marley's body up. Dallas had also paid Mack to collect the surveillance tapes in the ballroom. When the police had gotten there, Arlington fed them some bullshit story about sending the tapes on ahead with another investigator; they believed him with no problem. Dallas wanted to dislike Morgan's father, but he had major clout. All of his help had given Dallas time to get the situation straightened out.   Mack   was the one person they could call no matter the situation. He disposed of any unwanted bodies, weapons, and vehicles that could possibly cause jail time. The hood kept his pockets fat; his services were priceless. This time, he'd been paid to collect Marley as well as alter the footage and get it sent to the police department with minimum suspicion. Overall it had been a long day, and all Dallas had to do now was get all of the women home and safe.   He   and   Morgan both needed rest. From the talk he'd just had with Tasheena, she needed some rest as well. He gathered Morgan, Lay-Lay, and Tasheena, and left the hotel. After dropping Lay-Lay and Tasheena off at home, he and Morgan headed back to her place. Once they were settled in, he could tell she was distraught so he fed her, bathed her, and put her to bed. He showered once she was settled and joined her in bed.

*****

It was the middle of the night when Morgan woke up. The twins were making her very uncomfortable and she had to pee. When she rolled over, she realized Dallas was no longer in the bed with her. She lay there for a second, trying to make herself move. The lower part of her body was in serious pain. The twins were definitely making themselves some room.

While willing her body to move, Morgan thought back on her conversation with her father from earlier. After everything had gone down, before he and D. Karter left, Morgan pulled him to the side demanding answers. He promised her that he and D. Karter would be flying back in a few hours after taking care of their business, and they could have dinner and talk then.

Morgan knew this may be a bit too soon, but she wanted to get everything out in the open so they could all move on. Dallas needed just as many answers from his father as she needed from hers. Hopefully their dads would be open minded and honest. She hadn't told Dallas about their dinner plans yet, but she prayed he went along with them. Morgan lay in deep thought for a few seconds before turning over to her side. She rolled and shifted, trying to relieve some of the pressure from the twins. After a few minutes, she was able to get out of bed.   Once she handled her business in the bathroom, she went to the living room to check for Dallas. He was lying in the middle of the floor, watching her ceiling fan turn. Just like Morgan, he loved that spot. For some reason, watching the blades of the fan spin was relaxing.

"Come lay down with me." Dallas looked up to see Morgan leaning against the wall holding her belly.

She looked so beautiful. Pregnancy looked great on Morgan. He made a mental note to keep her pregnant. He smiled inwardly, thinking of how she would feel about that idea. He'd always wanted a lot of kids. Hopefully every time he got her pregnant, it would be with twins. The short gown she was wearing was hiked up some in the front due to her protruding tummy. Dallas' eyes traveled up her long legs and stopped at her thighs. He scooted backwards some, trying to see up her gown, but she backed up.

She walked towards him. "You are so nasty."

Dallas tried to make her straddle his face, but she pushed his hands away. Dallas was in the mood for sex, but apparently she wasn't. Morgan eased down slowly until she was lying beside him on the floor. With her head on his chest, she rubbed his stomach with her other hand.

"You thinking about D. Karter?"

"Yeah. I'm also thinking about Arlington Taylor. I got to see what's up with those two niggas, man. I know that's your daddy and everything Morgan, but I'm not really feeling his ass right now. All of this shit is so fucked up. I don't know what way is the right way. Only thing that I'm sure of is you. I don't want you getting hurt mentally or physically. I especially don't want my babies stressed out. I think you need to chill. Worry about the babies and let me handle this from here on out."

"Okay. As long as I can go to dinner later today with the both of them, then I'll chill. I want answers just like you do."

"Trust me, I'll get us some answers, but right now all I want to get is some of my goodies." Dallas positioned himself over Morgan and cupped her moist center with his hand.

She squirmed from the contact and opened her legs for him. Dallas kissed down her body, making her wetter. He wasn't able to earlier, but now he was about to take his time. He couldn't get enough of Morgan's body. Her warmth eased his mind. He told her he loved her over and over as they made love.

Chapter 12

The two pink lines showed up clear as day. She had already taken two, and all three test confirmed the same thing. She was indeed pregnant. Jade plopped down on the toilet and stared at the three sticks lined up on the counter. She had been nauseated for the past couple of days, and hadn't seen her period in almost two months.

She hadn't wanted to believe it, but there certainly was no denying it now. Although she knew her and King hadn't been using any forms of birth control, she wasn't sure she was ready. Initially she'd wanted to get birth control, but changed her mind. She'd heard too many horror stories from various females about it. There was a different story for every birth control method she'd given thought to. After a while, she just figured they could play it safe, and nothing would happen. So much for that theory. Jade stared at the tests a few more times before getting up to brush her teeth. King would be up for work in a minute, and she didn't want him to know yet–at least, not until she figured out how she felt about it first. She wasn't sure she would be able to handle it if he felt anything like she did right now. It wasn't that she didn't want the pregnancy, it was just shocking and scary. She had just finished washing her face when the bathroom door opened. She scrambled to grab the tests, but she wasn't sure if she was fast enough.

"Since when do you close doors?" King put the toilet seat up to pee.

He and Jade lived alone, and they never closed doors. There was no need to. They didn't have anything to hide from the other; they were a very open couple.

"I didn't want to wake you up." Jade looked at King; she couldn't tell if he believed her or not, so she didn't say anything. Once he finished, he washed his hands and followed her into their bedroom.

"I think I want a boy. We can name him King Jr." Jade turned around. Her face was filled with alarm. "Jade, you had to know I saw those damn tests in your hand." He smiled and walked over to rub her stomach. "Your stomach is a little pudgier than normal. I noticed it weeks ago. Your breasts are getting huge as fuck too. I notice everything about you. I probably know your body better than you do. I'm sure you knew I already had an idea about our baby. I mean I wasn't sure, but I had my suspicions."

He was so happy. She watched a smile spread across his face as he massaged her abdomen. "You happy?"

"I am now. I didn't know if you wanted kids yet. I know your mama and daddy are going to be on cloud nine when we tell them."

King laughed, because she was right. Karen and OJ were going to worry her to death about this baby.

Especially Karen. His mom already loved her to death, and now that she was carrying his baby, her happiness was about to shoot through the roof. King kissed all over Jade's shoulders as she sat on the bed. She was scrolling through the Internet on the phone, looking for a good OB doctor. She'd called the place Morgan went to and set up an appointment. She looked to the side and saw King sitting there staring at her. She laughed at his excitement. He was acting like a child on their birthday. Once her appointment was confirmed, she hung up and smiled.

"Baby, we're going to be parents." She lunged towards him. He caught her and sat her back down on the bed.

"Don't be jumping around acting all wild and shit. You're pregnant, so act like it and sit your ass down somewhere." Jade laughed so hard tears came down her face.

King laughed with her as he began to dress for work. Jade could already see this was about to be a long nine months.

*****

The plane ride back to Atlanta was a tedious one. D. Karter could hardly sit still. He had been waiting for this moment for as long as he could remember, and it was finally about to happen. Judging by Dallas' actions yesterday, this meeting wasn't going to go as smoothly as he hoped. Looking back over the way things went, D.

Karter couldn't blame him. Dallas had thought he was dead all of that time, then he showed up out of thin air. D. Karter looked over at Arlington. He looked as cool as a cucumber. That was one thing he admired about his friend, he never seemed bothered by anything. The only thing that could get a rise out of him was his family.

Initially, D. Karter was angry that Arlington hadn't bothered to tell him that it was his daughter that Dallas was dating. When he brought up the issue to Arlington, he just shrugged his shoulders. Arlington had always been a very private and protective man. After he explained that he wanted to keep Morgan under the radar, D. Karter let the situation go.

Two hours later, their plane landed and they were headed to the restaurant. Morgan had texted Arlington letting him know she and Dallas would be there shortly. They had just enough time to change before going to meet them. D. Karter hadn't been aware of their plans until that morning. Arlington told him about him and Morgan's talk and how she wanted explanations. Being that they had a few more things to handle in Atlanta anyway, Arlington figured the dinner couldn't do too much more damage. D. Karter agreed; maybe it would help more than it would hurt.

Once again, Morgan and father were on the same page without knowing. She was just as worried about how the dinner was going to turn out as he was. Albeit neither of them knew the other was worried, they were once again in sync unknowingly. She and Dallas were in his truck on their way to the restaurant to meet with their fathers. Dallas was looking out of the window and not saying much, which made Morgan a little uneasy. She couldn't quite gauge his mood, being that he wasn't talking.

"I don't even know how all of this is going to turn out. I hope they don't kill each other." Morgan was on the phone with Jade and Lay-Lay. She'd been on the phone with them for the last two hours discussing yesterday's horrific events. Jade was blown away. Being that Lay-Lay had been there most of the time, she was pretty cool.

"Y'all better not be up in that restaurant acting a fool, Morgan. I don't have the time or the bail money to be getting y'all out of jail."

"Jade please! They will be in jail by themselves. What I look like sitting my big butt in jail?"

"I can't stand when hoes get pregnant and immediately start referring to themselves as big. Morgan bye. Your ass probably ain't in nothing but a size five. I haven't been that small since elementary school."

Jade and Morgan both laughed at Lay-Lay as she continued to joke on Morgan's pregnancy weight. They conversed the rest of the way to Ruth's Chris Steakhouse before hanging up. Morgan stole glances at Dallas as they walked into the building. She could tell he was nervous. Morgan grabbed his hand and gave it a light squeeze. As the waiter showed them to their table, Morgan said a silent prayer that everything would go smoothly. When they got to their table Arlington and D. Karter were already there. Morgan hugged them both before sitting in the chair Dallas had pulled out for her. He hadn't said anything yet. She wasn't even sure he'd made eye contact with either of the men.

Morgan looked around the table, and everybody's eyes were on somebody. She smiled and tried to make small talk about the menu. When she got nothing but grunts and hardly any answers, she got mad. She was not about to sit at a table filled with grown men, and let them act like children. They all looked to be so caught up in other things, so she decided to test them. She'd get all of their attention one way or the other. When the waitress came back to take their drink orders, Morgan asked for a Tropical Margarita and a tall glass of bud light. All three of them opened their mouths to speak, but Dallas' words came out first.

"Morgan, you're not about to drink that shit!"

"So now y'all see me? I couldn't tell a minute ago." She looked at all of them one by one.

Her father smiled. Morgan was indeed his daughter. "I'm sorry, baby girl. I just wanted to give your young friend the chance to speak to his father. I thought maybe they should hash things out first."

Dallas shifted in his seat so that he was now sitting closer to the table. "Sir don't disrespect me again. You know my fucking name, so use it."

Morgan gasped at his outburst. She looked at him with her brows furrowed and her lips pressed into a straight line. Her eyes pleaded with him to be a little nicer. When Dallas noticed how disgruntled she was, he felt a tinge of guilt and wished he could take his words back. He knew how much Morgan loved her father, and in no way did he want to cause her any pain or discomfort. He was about to ease back some until he noticed Arlington's unwavering eyes were still on him.

Dallas and Arlington shot daggers at one another with their eyes. Arlington retreated first, because he didn't want to upset Morgan.

"Dallas, don't take your anger out on Arlington. It's me you're angry with. Let's address it."

Morgan looked from Dallas to D. Karter. They were staring each other down. Morgan rubbed Dallas' thigh beneath the table to give him the push he needed. He stopped her movement when he grabbed her hand and held it.

"I don't know you. I don't want to know you. I'm not even sure why you're here. You left when I was a child. I'm a man now, I don't need you, so feel free to back off."

Dallas' words came out sharp as a knife. Morgan was sure they cut Karter deep, but he deserved it. Dallas was right. He nodded his head and spoke anyway.

"Dallas, the choices I've made were to protect you and Marcy. The business I'm in was too dangerous for a man with a family. The problem was, by the time you came I was already in too deep to quit. Leaving you wasn't my first choice, but it was the best one. Being a father and a husband means more than just having a woman and children. That title holds weight, son. When you take on those two things, you're changing your life forever. You're putting your needs and wants on hold for theirs." Dallas was sitting straight up in his chair with his eyes glued to D. Karter. He wanted to hear what it was that his father had to say for himself.

"Sure I wanted to stay with Marcy and raise you. Hell yes, I wanted to be a part of everything you've become, but you and your mother's safety came before what I wanted. I couldn't put you all in harm's way because I wanted to be there. Had I not left when I did, my being there wouldn't have mattered, because you all would be gone. Marcy was attacked and you were taken. You probably don't remember, because you were sleeping, but the streets bled that night. Between Arty and I, no one involved made it to daylight. I did everything I could so when you woke up the next morning, you'd be back in your bed. If I hadn't had

• • •

Arlington's help, there is no telling what would have happened. So when you speak to him, speak with respect."

Morgan shifted some in her seat, a little bothered by the intensity of D. Karter's words. She looked around the table, and her father looked like his normal composed self, sitting slightly slouched in his chair and sipping his sweet tea. Dallas' eyes were a tad bit glossy, while D. Karter's were focused and staunch. His body language was that of tenacity and assurance. He looked over at Morgan briefly, and he winked before continuing his one-sided conversation with Dallas.

"As far as our relationship goes, I hope we can salvage what's left. I make my final take down next week and I'll be retiring. I would love to be a part of my grandchildren's lives as well as yours. Dallas, you may not understand my choices but as a man, you will respect them. You are grown. You have Morgan and she has your babies. Their wellbeing comes before yours. There will come a time when you have to make decisions your children and wife that you may not like, but it won't matter. As their protector, you'll do whatever is best. I see the way you look at Morgan now. The way you hold her and care for her. The look on your face when she ordered that alcohol a second ago was priceless. It shows me you love her, and you love your children. Just for a minute Dallas, imagine the depths you would go to in order to keep them safe, and know that's exactly what I did for you and your mother."

Morgan was blown away by everything D. Karter had just said. She cried silently as she listened to him. She knew he was sincere, and she wanted Dallas to forgive him. If Dallas was half the man his father was, she'd chosen right. Morgan knew in her mind this was nothing she had to worry about. Dallas showed her that on a daily basis. She had no idea her father was as deeply involved in this type of lifestyle, but in a weird way, she was proud of him. He was fiercely loyal, and she loved it. She continued holding Dallas' hand until he excused himself. She got up and followed him out of the door. He was standing on the sidewalk with his hands in his pockets. He was looking up towards the sky with moist eyes.

"Everything will be okay, Dally. It'll take some time, but it'll all work itself out." Morgan linked her arm through his and leaned her head on his shoulder. Dallas let out a loud sigh.

"Morgan, I'm angry because he's right. I'm so mad at him for leaving, but I understand. I hated him, then I missed him, then I ended up hating him again. I have so many emotions going on inside right now, and I don't know how to handle them. I want to be mad, but I have no reason to be." Dallas turned to face Morgan and grabbed the bottom of her face with his hand. He looked deep into her eyes and saw the love. "I'm willing to give him a chance because of you. Had I never met you and realized what real love is, I wouldn't understand those type of sacrifices." Dallas placed his hand over Morgan's stomach. "If it meant keeping you and these two safe, I'd leave tomorrow and never look back. Thank God I don't have to do that, but I would. I love you."

Morgan couldn't stop the tears from falling. What had she done so right in her life to deserve such a man? Dallas grabbed her in a hug so tight she could feel his heartbeat. She didn't know how long they'd been hugging, but by the time they stopped, both of their fathers were outside. Morgan kissed Dallas' lips and pushed him towards D. Karter as she walked to her father. When she got to Arlington, he told her all about how he'd tolerated Dallas' behavior only for tonight, and only for her. He disclosed that although he hated to admit it, he admired Dallas. Dallas was a very bold and respectable man. Dallas hadn't taken any slack from him or D. Karter since they'd met. He could have very easily let all of this run him over for Morgan's sake, but he hadn't. Dallas stood strong, and held firm like a man was supposed to. Once all of this blew over, Arlington was going to have to let Morgan know he approved of her choice. He also admired the special care Dallas took with his daughter.

Arlington wrapped his arm around Morgan's shoulder and removed the toothpick from his mouth.

"Your mother would be very pleased with the newfound boldness in you."

"It's because of Dallas."

"This I know. You're his weakness, as he's your strength. That's how it should be, sweetheart. That's the perfect combination for an everlasting love."

Arlington kissed the top of Morgan's head and whispered in her ear how happy he was that she'd found Dallas. Morgan was so happy to have her father's approval; it meant everything to her. They stood there watching Dallas as he walked towards D. Karter. He was moving slowly, but he was getting there. When he was close enough, D. Karter grabbed him in a hug. Dallas didn't hug him back right away, but when he finally did, it was beautiful. Morgan wanted to jump up and down, but she was sure all three of the men would have a problem with that. They hugged for a while until Dallas finally pulled away. Morgan let their fathers know she was happy everything worked out, and they would see them later. Arlington told her he loved her before he and D. Karter turned to leave. Before they got too far, he heard Morgan talking again.

"I hope to see you both one day soon. Maybe then, everybody will be more comfortable, and we can enjoy ourselves. If not, I'll understand." Morgan blew both men kisses. "I love you, Daddy."

Morgan walked slowly back to Dallas so that they could leave. When she was only a few feet away from him, he grabbed her hand and led her to the car. He held it to his mouth and kissed it before opening the door for her. Once they were in and settled, he pulled off. Morgan looked out of the window as they drove. The silence in the car was actually welcomed. Nothing about it seemed awkward at all; he was thinking, and so was she.   Her hand was still in his as he drove. From the direction they were going, she could tell he wasn't taking her home just yet. She looked over at him and was about to ask where they were going, but was caught off guard. His eyes were wet, and a few tears were rolling down his face.

"Aww Dally don't cry. What's wrong baby?" He shook his head.

"Something is wrong, Dallas. Is it your dad? Everything will get better, babe."

"It's not that M. I mean that's not all it is…it's all of this. Everything. Him, my memory, you and the babies. Just everything."

Morgan's heart went out to him. This stuff couldn't have been easy for him. Plainly putting it, it was stress all wrapped in one. It all was enough to make a weaker man go crazy. She rubbed his thigh as he drove. Words, and even sentences and phrases popped into her mind. She wanted to say something, anything, that would make him feel better or to at least lighten the load, but there wasn't anything.

"I love you Dallas, and I think you're the most beautiful and awesome man I've ever met. You make me want to be so much more. Everything that I am today is because of you. When I first met you, I was pretty bad ass." She watched him smile. "But now I'm more than that. You bring out the best in me, and I cannot wait to birth our kids. I know they're going to be perfect for me, just like their father."

When he turned his head to look at her, the love he felt was indescribable. All of the feelings he had for her were on the forefront; they was seeping through his eyes.

"I love you so much Morgan, damn," his voice sounded weak. "I love you too much." He shook his head and raised her hand to kiss it again.

"We'll be all right Dallas. As long as I have you, then I'm good."

"Ditto baby mama. Ditto." Morgan laughed before snatching her hand away.

"I ain't your damn baby mama. I hate that shit. I'm your girlfriend and I'm having your kids. End of discussion." Morgan crossed her arms over her chest. "I need to be mad at you anyway for making me a damn baby mama. I ain't never wanted to be in no mess like this. I'm wife material nigga, and you've just demoted me to a damn baby mama." Morgan got mad that fast. She'd always had plans for her life that she'd stuck to before she met Dallas. She threw caution to the wind when it came to him. Now she was knocked up.

"Don't sit over there and make this about you. I'm stressed about my dad." Dallas' tone was filled with humor.

"Don't play with me, Dallas. Fuck your daddy. He here now, take his ass and be happy," Morgan snapped.

Dallas laughed. "Damn. You mad for real, huh?"

"I'm not mad. Just disappointed. I didn't want to be a baby mama, Dallas," Morgan stated crying. "And I'm ready to have these damn babies. I'm tired of crying all the time."

The look on Dallas' face was priceless. He looked like he really didn't understand why she was so distraught.

"Chill Morgan. It's not that serious, girl. Daddy will make it better. Okay?" He ran his hand over her belly.

Morgan nodded her head and tried to catch her breath as her crying subsided.

"You trust me?"

"Yes."

"Well stop all that crying. I got you. You never left me, so you have to know I'm never leaving you. No matter what. Boyfriend and girlfriend, baby mama, baby daddy. Whatever we are, I'll be here."

"Okay," she spoke softly. Morgan looked back out of the window and rubbed her stomach. The babies were moving all over the place. She grabbed Dallas' hand and placed it over her stomach. "Feel right here, that's a head." She scooted his hand lower until it was completely under her belly.

"Damn what's that?" Dallas rubbed his hand around the spot she'd placed it in.

"That's one of their spines. It feels funny huh? Their back is pressed against my stomach, that's why it's so hard. It might be one of their little butts, I don't really know." Morgan smiled at her stomach.

"This pregnancy shit is too fucking crazy. Your body do all kinds of weird stuff. It's almost like you're a fish bowl."

Morgan frowned her face up. "A fish bowl Dallas, really?"

"Yeah. You're the bowl and you have little fish swimming around in your stomach. They flip and float and shit." Dallas was laughing at his own analogy.

He was laughing so hard that Morgan had to laugh too. This boy was a damn fool with his silly ass.

"I can't with you right now, Mr. Streeter."

"Well I can with you Mrs. Streeter, hell I can with you anytime. Right now, tomorrow, next week, shit forever. You and me...we never ending."

"I know baby. I know."

● ● ●

178

Morgan looked at her man and smiled. He was her stress reliever. Every ounce of stress she'd just been feeling moments ago was gone. Hopefully this was a feeling that would remain until the world blew.

Chapter 13

Dallas watched Morgan sleep. He couldn't imagine ever living a life without her and their babies. She looked so peaceful and he didn't want to wake her, so he left. He had gotten dressed and was about to meet up with King and Smoke. After the meeting with his father, he felt relieved. He'd talked to his mother last night, and she confirmed everything his father said. She let him know that his father had been there since the beginning. He didn't understand how he never once saw him, but his mother promised he was at everything. She begged him to forgive her for keeping his father's presence a secret, but she promised him that she'd only done it to keep him safe. Morgan also confirmed he'd visited him every night while he was in the hospital. Morgan had convinced him to give both of their fathers another chance. Dallas was actually excited about starting over.

When he parked outside the store, he spotted King and Smoke on the sidewalk. He dapped them both up and they headed inside. Dallas was floored. King had said the man was legit, but he didn't know it was to this extent. Diamonds were everywhere. How in the hell was he about to choose one. He was glad King and Smoke were there. They helped him narrow his choices down until he'd found the perfect one. It was a dark blue

• • •

diamond that was shaped like a square. It had small clear stones surrounding it. It was perfect–Morgan would love it.

Smoke slapped Dallas on his back. "Y'all niggas make me feel bad."

"You should. If your ass would have left Kristen alone, you would be in the same boat."

"Nah, see that's where you're wrong. Even if I had, which I still haven't, I wouldn't be up in here. I'm not ready for marriage. Hell nah! The same pussy forever? I can't even imagine it." Smoke shook like he was cold.

Dallas and King laughed at him before Dallas went to the register to pay for the ring. Just as they prepared to leave. Dallas got a text from Morgan.

Morgan: Miss you
Dallas: Miss y'all too. I'll be there in a few
Morgan: K. Love you.
Dallas: I love y'all too. Go eat!
Morgan: Yes sir daddy ☺

Dallas stuck his phone in his pocket and headed to his truck.

Once he got home, Morgan was in the kitchen making breakfast. She wore panties and one of his tank tops. Her stomach was getting bigger, and he loved it. Her belly button looked funny sticking out of his shirt, but he even liked that. Today Morgan had an appointment for them to find out the sex of the babies, and he couldn't wait. He walked up and wrapped his arms around her waist and kissed her neck. She turned to the side so she could kiss his mouth.

"Don't be sneaking up on me. I could have had my other baby daddy up in here."

"I ain't worried about that. I'd beat his ass and make him watch me fuck his fine ass baby mama." Dallas slapped her on her butt and walked away.

Morgan was still laughing at him when her cell phone rang. It was Jade. She wanted to know could her and Lay-Lay go to the appointment to see what she was having. After Morgan told them yes and the time of her appointment, they hung up. She finished breakfast and set the table. She hadn't told Dallas yet, but she'd invited their fathers over to eat with them. Once she was finished, she ran into the room to change into something more appropriate. No sooner than she had finished putting on her clothes did the doorbell ring. Dallas stuck his head out of the closet and asked who was at the door. Morgan smiled and left. When he finally got into the kitchen, he was caught off guard. He hadn't talked to his father more than once or twice since their dinner at Ruth's Chris.

D. Karter stuck his hand out for a shake. "Good morning son." Dallas hugged him instead.

Morgan and Arlington were so happy the two were making progress. Although Morgan was skeptical at first, breakfast went pretty good. Everybody talked and laughed the entire time. Dallas and D. Karter talked about Dallas' childhood while Morgan and Arlington talked about hers. Once everyone had finished eating, they bid their goodbyes until next time. Arlington and D. Karter were both flying out of Atlanta that day, so they wouldn't see each other again for a little while. Morgan thought Dallas would be upset with her for not telling him about their surprise breakfast guests, but he wasn't. He actually thanked her. The next few hours passed as they lay around the house. By the time it was time to go to her doctor, Morgan was bubbling over with excitement. As they walked out to the car, Jade, Lay-Lay, King, and Smoke were pulling up. They followed Dallas and Morgan to the doctor's office.

Morgan headed for the front of the building with all of them in tow. "Damn y'all act like I couldn't just call and tell y'all the sexes."

"Morgan shut up, you know you're happy we're here," Jade smiled as she rubbed Morgan's belly.

When they walked into the office, Morgan checked in and waited to be called. The nurse was surprised to see so many people following Morgan. She told them normally she wouldn't have done that, but she was feeling nice that day, so she allowed them all to come into the room with Morgan. The room was so small that they were all crammed in, practically falling over each other. There were two chairs along the wall that Jade and Lay-Lay were sitting in. King, and Smoke stood closely beside them. Half of Smoke's body was hidden behind the Ultrasound machine. Once everybody had gotten semi-comfortable, she began the visit. It took her a while to get to the part everyone was waiting for. She went through all of the measurements, slowly building the suspense.

"Okay, now for the part we've all been waiting for," she smiled at the group. "Any preferences?"

Everybody wanted two boys except Jade and Morgan. They wanted two girls.

"Well let's see." The nurse rolled the monitor around stopping on twin A.

"Dad, we have your boy!" The room filled with cheers and comments.

She moved over to twin B. After a little more moving, she stopped again.

"Mom, here's your little mini me. It's a girl."

Jade and Morgan gushed with excitement. The men made jokes with Dallas about having to shoot men in the future about his baby girl, while the nurse printed the ultrasound photos out. King kissed Jade's cheek and let her know he couldn't wait for their baby to get there. They'd decided against telling anybody yet because Jade didn't want to intrude on Morgan's time. She wanted everything to be all about Morgan for the time being; it would be her time soon enough. When Morgan was all cleaned up, the nurse came back and handed her the photos. Morgan was so happy as she flipped through the pictures. When she got to the last one, she stopped. She stared at it for a long time before her eyes started to water. Everyone in the room was watching her. When Lay-Lay saw she was about to cry, she walked up to her.

"What's wrong?"

Morgan shook her head, unable to speak. When Morgan finally looked up from the picture, Lay-Lay had moved and was standing next to everyone else. The only person that was next to her was Dallas. He was kneeling in front of her with the ring he'd bought earlier. The nurse had printed the words **Will You Marry Our Daddy?** on the last ultrasound. Morgan hadn't thought her life could get any better; she'd been wrong. She nodded yes, because she was too overwhelmed to speak. Dallas slid the ring on her finger as all of her friends applauded.

"No wonder all y'all asses wanted to tag along today. Y'all set me up." Morgan wiped her face with the back of her arm.

Jade passed her some tissue. "It was only right after how y'all did me."

Jade smiled as she and Lay-Lay ran over to check out her ring. When they exited the room, there were balloons and a *Congratulations* banner hanging across the waiting room. Morgan's tears continued to flow. Her eyes were so clouded with tears she could hardly see. Dallas had his arms wrapped around her waist as he stood behind her. He didn't let her go until they'd walked outside and were back at his truck.

Lay-Lay squealed with excitement as she wrapped her arm around Morgan. "I'm so happy for you bestie."

Jade followed suit. King, Smoke, and Dallas watched as the women shared in Morgan's excitement. They took turns taking pictures and kissing Morgan's belly. After another ten minutes, Dallas went to help Morgan into the truck. When she opened the door, there was a bouquet of red roses with a card. Morgan turned around to find everybody still watching.

"Y'all showing out now."

"Girl hush and open the damn card." Lay-Lay smacked Smoke upside his head as soon as the words left his mouth.

"Dallas is this real? You can't be serious right now." Morgan dropped the card containing their flight itinerary onto the ground and jumped on him. He grabbed her quickly and held onto her tightly.

"Chill your ass out girl. Don't be shaking my babies up." Morgan kissed all over his smiling face.

"I can't help it, I'm just so happy."

"WE'RE GOING TO CABO!" Jade and Lay-Lay screamed.

Dallas had his mom book the trip the day he'd found out Morgan was pregnant. After talking with

Smoke that day, he knew he needed to make it up to her. Although he'd paid for the trip, he'd made sure to get insurance on it just in case the dates he chose didn't work for her. After everything with their father's had gone down, he figured now was as good as time as any. He, King, and Smoke had gone to the travel agency the day before and arranged for them to use their reserved voucher. When Dallas informed King and Smoke of his plans, they dropped a few stacks and were able to book them and their girls some spots on the trip as well.

Dallas didn't want to wait any longer to marry his girl. Jade and Lay-Lay had packed all the bags, and their flight was leaving in four hours. Morgan squeezed Dallas' neck with all the strength she could muster. After that, the group left and headed for the airport. They made it just in time to check their bags and board the plane.

*****

Morgan's toes felt good in the sand as she and her father walked down the aisle. He and her mother had surprised her and flown straight to Cabo for the wedding. They'd gotten there yesterday and were waiting at the airport when they arrived. When her mother told her about Dallas buying them round trip tickets there, she cried like a baby; she was so happy. The sight before her was too beautiful for words. Dallas, King, and Smoke were all dressed in white while Jade,

Lay-Lay, and Hannah were dressed in dark purple. The only person missing was Kyle, but sadly he couldn't make it due to work.

John Legend's voice carried across the beach as he sang *Stay with You*. That had been Morgan's favorite song from the first time she'd heard it. Now it was her wedding day, and Dallas had gotten him there to sing it just for her; she was so happy. Morgan couldn't stop smiling as she made her way to the man of her dreams. She loved Dallas more than life itself. He had come into her life and made her the happiest woman on the planet. The tears in his eyes proved to her that he felt the same. He grabbed her hand and helped her onto the platform. Her pearl white maternity gown blew in the wind as she stepped forward. After her father kissed her cheek, he went to stand by her mother. The entire wedding went by beautifully, and Morgan couldn't have been happier.

*****

Smoke walked up to Lay-Lay on the sandy area that was designated for dancing. "Lay-Lay you know we're next."

"Nigga please! You know I don't fuck with you like that."

"Damn, that's fucked up Lay-Lay."

"Smoke stop it. We're cool, but I'm not worried about you. You don't want me like I want you, so let's just be friends."

With that, Lay-Lay smiled and walked away. She loved Smoke, but he wasn't ready to change. It hurt, but she was dealing with it. After seeing the trouble King and Dallas went through to make Jade and Morgan happy, it showed her she deserved better. He was their friend, but he was nothing like them. He was a ho, plain and simple. In the back of her mind, she knew they weren't over. They did this all the time—break up to make up. She'd catch him later after she'd had a few more drinks. Lay-Lay walked over to where King and Jade were sitting and sat down. She poured herself a glass of the champagne that was on the table.

"Jay, why you ain't drinking?" King had just held up his cup for Lay-Lay to refill.

"I just don't want none."

"Girl it's a party. You better drink. I know I'm about to get lit baby." Lay-Lay laughed as she pushed her glass up to Jade's lips. Jade swatted her hand.

"Stop bitch, I said I don't want none."

Lay-Lay looked at Jade before sitting her glass down on the table. When she turned around, she pointed her finger in Jade's face.

"King dun' fucked around and knocked your ass up, hasn't he? You're sitting up here pregnant as Morgan's ass is, aren't you?"

Jade looked around to make sure nobody had heard Lay-Lay. Luckily it was only her, King and Lay-Lay that had heard. Once satisfied that no one else was listening, she turned back around and faked confusion. "What?"

"Nah bitch, don't what me. I know you are, because you're my drinking partner. I know Morgan's ass will tap out, but not you. I'm Nemo, and you're Dory, we drink like fish my nigga. Your ole pregnant ass." Jade and King both laughed at Lay-Lay.

"Shalaya, you are so fucking silly. Yeah I'm pregnant. But why I got to be Dory? How you get to be Nemo?" Lay-Lay jumped up and down smiling. She was so happy for her friend.

"Now I get to be an auntie three times. At the rate you and Morgan are going, I don't ever have to have kids."

Jade and Lay-Lay continued laughing and talking until Morgan walked over to them. Dallas and Smoke were right behind her. The rest of the night went by, and the friends enjoyed each other.

*****

By two o clock, everybody had gone back to their rooms. Morgan couldn't sleep, so she called Jade and Lay-Lay to go back down to the beach with her. She had been so caught up with Dallas the last couple of months they hadn't spent a lot of time together. She missed her sisters.

"Morgan, did you know I'm about to have three babies?" Lay-Lay started in as soon as she sat down.

"What girl? I know you ain't let Smoke's dog ass get you pregnant." Morgan jerked her head back and frowned at Lay-Lay.

Lay-Lay rolled her eyes to the sky. "Shut up Morgan with your slow ass. I'm talking about Jade."

Morgan turned around and punched Jade in the arm. "I should slap you. Why you ain't tell me?"

"I was just about to, until loud ass over here opened up her mouth."

Morgan was so happy. Now Jade would finally have her own little family. They stayed on the beach until the sun came up.

*****

Three weeks later. . .

It was a beautiful day, and it had been a beautiful month. Morgan and Dallas had been honeymooning like crazy. You'd think they would be used to each other by now, being that they'd been together a couple of months shy of two years. They weren't, their love was still fresh. Being husband and wife had taken their life to a new level. Every five minutes, they were kissing or touching. The word happy was an understatement for these two.

Morgan sat on the weight bench in Dallas' garage as he worked out. The six-month lease on her apartment was now up, so she moved in with him. He was busy doing push-ups while she watched. The sweat dripping down the muscles in his back was driving her crazy. She sat back on the bench and crossed her legs tightly. Dallas had her dripping wet, and he wasn't even touching her.

"Uncross those legs. Daddy gon' give you what you need in a minute."
Morgan looked at her fingernails, trying to suppress the smile on her face. "What?"
"Don't what me. I know a nigga got that pussy juicing up. I see you crossing your legs all tight and shit. Let me finish working out, and I'll have this dick hard and ready for you." He didn't even look at her as he continued with his pull ups.
Morgan was at a loss for words. Dallas was so nasty, but he knew her so well. She wasn't even aware he had been paying any attention to her. Instead of continuing to torture herself, she got up and removed her clothing. Midway through, Dallas had stopped to watch her. She didn't have time to wait. Her baby shower was today and she needed some sex so she could go. She had two hours before it started, and she hadn't taken a shower or anything. Dallas got the hint

and grabbed a towel to dry himself off. Morgan quickly snatched it from him. She wanted him just the way he was. His smelly, sweaty body turned her on. Within seconds, they were devouring each other. Dallas bent her over and fucked her senseless. When they were done, they retreated into the house to get ready.

*****

"It's about time you got here." Morgan looked up at Kyle.

He'd just walked in the door. Morgan's shower had been going on for almost an hour, and he was just getting there. The room was decorated in purple, light green, and yellow. Marcy and Hannah had outdone themselves. Between the two of them, they had gotten on Morgan's nerves. Every other day one of them was calling about decorations, food, or games. Most of the ideas she'd had, they'd decided against and gone with their own. She was so glad the day had gotten there and was about to be over. She and Dallas' moms had done so much that there was nothing left for Jade and Lay-Lay to do.

Kyle kissed the top of her head. "I'm sorry sis. I got here as soon as I could."

He then moved to the side to shake Dallas' hand. It was then that Morgan noticed the woman behind him. She was a tall brown-skinned girl with long weave. Her face was contoured for the gods, and her figure was hot. She was definitely something to look at. She must have felt Morgan's eyes on her, because she turned her head and smiled.

"Hello Morgan, I'm Alissa. Kyle has told me so much about you all. I'm so happy to finally meet you." Morgan smiled as she accepted her outstretched hand.

"Nice to meet you, Alissa. I'm glad you could make it."

Morgan was smiling, but her mind was doing numbers. She hadn't heard not one thing about Miss Alissa. She was going to have to have a talk with Kyle. He hadn't mentioned he was seeing someone, let alone bringing her to family functions. Once Alissa was back next to Kyle, Morgan scanned the room for Lay-Lay. She and Kyle weren't together, but she knew this would upset her. Thankfully she hadn't seen them yet. She and Jade were busy hosting one of the games. Morgan gave Kyle a questioning look before nodding her head towards Lay-Lay. He shrugged his shoulders before walking away to sit down. She hadn't told Lay he was coming because she wanted it to be a surprise; now she wished she would have. This was about to be one hell of a surprise.

*****

"Winner takes All—" Lay-Lay was announcing the winner when her eyes locked with Kyles. Her heart skipped a beat, because she hadn't known he was coming. She had to stop herself from smiling as he winked at her. She turned her head and went back to the game. She couldn't wait to finish so she could go talk to him. After another fifteen minutes, the game was over and Lay-Lay was headed to the restroom. She needed to freshen up. When she was sure she looked fine, she exited. The hallway was a short one, but it was dark. It was so dark she hadn't even seen Smoke standing there until he spoke.

"I miss you Lay-Lay." Lay stumbled backwards and fell against the wall.

"Damn Smoke, you scared the shit out of me." She was holding her chest trying to steady her heartbeat.

"I'm sorry. I didn't mean to. I just wanted to catch you by yourself. I love you and I miss your ass like hell. I know I fucked up, but I promise to do better from now on. You're all I got. I'm in love with you, please give me another chance."

Lay-Lay couldn't believe her luck. Just when she was ready to finally let him go, here he comes with this shit. She loved Smoke, and wanted to be with him, but she wasn't sure how serious he was. He always apologized and went right back to doing the same thing, although this time he seemed a little more sincere. He'd been calling and texting nonstop since Morgan and Dallas' wedding. He'd even gone as far as to send a few gifts to her job and house, all of which were out of character for him.

"Smoke, why are you doing this?"

He shrugged his shoulders lazily, and looked from her to the ground. "I don't know. I'm tired of being without you. We belong together Lay-Lay. Just think about it."

"I'll think about it."

Lay-Lay was about to walk away when he pulled her to him for a hug. He held her so tight that she couldn't move. It felt so good to be in his arms again. She'd been acting mean, but she'd been missing Smoke something terrible. Smelling his scent had her rethinking letting him go in the first place. All she could think about was all the good times they'd had together.

"I love you, Jaylen." Lay-Lay rarely called him by his real name unless she was in her feelings. This was a bad sign. She only found herself calling him Jaylen when she was about to forgive him.

"I love you too Lay-Lay Ali." He pinched her butt before releasing her from his grip.

She walked away and back out to the party. She made eye contact with Kyle the moment she came out of the door. It was almost like he was staring at the door waiting for her to emerge. She couldn't read the look on his face. It looked nervous or sympathetic. She didn't know what to make of it–that was, until she noticed a pretty girl with long hair link her arm through his and kiss his ear. Lay-Lay stopped right in her tracks. That whole scene had caught her completely off guard. When she looked back into Kyle's face, he looked guilty. He wouldn't even make eye contact.

"Come on sis, help me fix Dallas and Morgan's plates."

Jade grabbed Lay-Lay and pulled her towards the food table. She and Morgan had been discussing Kyle's little friend while Lay-Lay was gone. They had watched everything from the other side of the room. Jade wanted to slap Kyle and that girl, but that wasn't her place. Lay-Lay followed Jade and helped her fix the food. Once they'd finished, she continued to busy herself. She organized gifts and entertained the guests. She made it her business not to look in Kyle's direction anymore. He and she weren't together. He didn't owe her anything.

Before long, it was time to open gifts. Lay-Lay leaned against the counter and watched as Dallas and Morgan smiled and held up the gifts for everyone to see. Morgan's stomach was in the way, so Dallas had to lean down and open the gifts before handing them to her. Lay watched as her best friend basked in happiness. On the other side of her, Jade was standing there taking pictures. King stood next to her, holding her water bottle and a plate of pineapples. Every so often, she would lean over and he would place some fruit into her mouth, or hold the water as she drank some. They were so in love, and it was beautiful.

Lay-Lay wasn't a hater by far, and she would most definitely never hate on her sisters. She still couldn't help feeling a little jealous. They both had found men that loved them unconditionally and treated them like queens. All she had was Smoke and his begging ass. She thought maybe she'd had Kyle, but obviously that ship had sailed. She wiped the tears that were threatening to fall from her eyes. *Lord please send me a man.* Lay-Lay prayed as she went to take pictures with everybody. Hopefully God would hear her and bless her with a man to give her all the things she deserved. Maybe, just maybe, it would be her turn next.

Text LEOSULLIVAN to 42828 to get a notification when PART THREE comes out!

Join our mailing list to get a notification when Leo Sullivan Presents has another release!

Text LEOSULLIVAN to 22828

to join!

Last release:

I'm in Love With a Thug 2

Check out our upcoming releases on the next page!

To submit a manuscript for our review, email us at leosullivanpresents@gmail.com

Join our mailing list to get a notification for these upcoming releases!

CPSIA information can be obtained
at www.ICGtesting.com
Printed in the USA
LVHW081830081219
639822LV00015B/836/P

9 781515 194255